D0341333

2'

92

7

2000
00
2000

JASPER AND HACK

They met in Yuma jail—a wild, good-natured, woman-loving ranny called Hack who had killed a man in a brawl, and a professional owlhooter called Jasper serving time after a payroll robbery that had gone badly wrong. When free again they met up by accident and became partners because at the time it seemed the best thing to do. But they were not as well-matched as they had thought, and they had opponents who were more dangerous than most: two old, hard-trailing law-bringers, and two professional killers who also had a score to settle.

JASPER
AND HACK

Jay Hill Potter

A Lythway Book

CHIVERS PRESS
BATH

First published in Great Britain 1981
by
Robert Hale Limited
This Large Print edition published by
Chivers Press
by arrangement with
Robert Hale Limited
1985

ISBN 0 7451 0144 5

British Library Cataloguing in Publication Data

Potter, Jay Hill
    Jasper and Hack.—Large print ed.—
    (A Lythway book)
    I. Title
    823'.914[F]   PR6066.O771

    ISBN 0–7451–0144–5

JASPER AND HACK

CHAPTER ONE

Hackwood was easing his pinto onto the trail which led to the big gates when the girl ran round the edge of the corral and called him.

He had been taking things slowly, half-expecting her. He reined in.

Panting, she clutched at his stirrup.

'You miserable skunk,' she gasped. 'You were running out on me.'

Her teeth gleamed. Her hair was wild.

'I said Goodnight,' he told her.

'What else could I do with your father watching?' he asked.

'You should've waited at the stables.'

'Your sweetheart was hanging around near there,' he said mockingly.

'Ned? I guess he was just watching for you to leave so he could go see Dad. You're not scared of Ned?'

Hackwood disregarded this half-question. He reached down and grabbed the girl with one arm around her back, his hand then sliding upwards almost to her armpit and touching the proud softness of her breast. He lifted her up to the saddle in front of him. She leaned back in his arms and they kissed.

Neither of them saw the man who came around the corner of the corral until he said

1

harshly, 'Get down, both of you.'

The girl jerked away from Hackwood and turned her head.

'Ned!'

'Get down I said. Both of you!'

'You followed me! You're spying on me! How...?'

'I have the right!' His voice was thick and trembling now. 'Get down. Or by God...' He left his sentence unfinished. The girl slid from the horse.

'You too, Hackwood.' The standing man's hand was very near to his gun. And the girl was in the way now.

'Happy to oblige you, suh,' said Hackwood mockingly. With slow and studied ease he got down from the saddle and stood beside his horse.

Ned glanced at the girl. 'Leave!' he said.

'Don't be foolish, Ned. I'm staying right here.'

'I'm not going to kill him,' Ned said. He was of finer build than Hackwood and younger. 'I'm just going to teach him a lesson.'

Hackwood laughed, a harsh sound without mirth. His thumbs were hooked in his belt.

Ned had moved... But the girl moved now also, and she was between them again.

'You fool,' she said to Ned. 'Come on. This is accomplishing nothing. I'll come back with you.'

2

'You'll go back alone!'

'I don't want to stand here gabbing all night,' put in Hackwood.

Ned took off his gunbelt and dropped it to the ground at his feet. 'Are you going to shoot me down now, bucko?' he jeered. 'Or have you got the guts to face me man to man without that shooter of yours?' He sounded steadier now, his rage in abeyance.

Deliberately, Hackwood took off his gunbelt and hung it over his saddle. 'Stand out of the way, girl.'

She turned on him. 'Get out of here, Hack!'

'I can't, girl. Move, please.'

'I will not!'

He strode forward, grabbed her by the shoulder and flung her to one side. She staggered, almost fell.

Ned rushed forward, his rage bursting forth again at Hackwood's treatment of the girl, Ned's girl. He flung a punch, but it was too hasty, misplaced. It only buffeted Hackwood's shoulder. It staggered him, however, knocking him in the opposite direction to the girl.

The impetus of Ned's rush and the blow he had flung carried him on—straight into Hackwood's balled fist, which sank into his belly just above the belt-buckle. Ned gulped and doubled forward. Hackwood brought his other arm over, the fist like a club. It smashed into the younger man's cheekbone and Ned

3

spun around twice before he fell.

He rolled onto his side.

His fingers scraped the grass and the soil as, stubbornly, he strove to rise.

Hackwood waited, his shoulders bent, his long arms hanging loosely, his hands half-claws.

The girl moved.

'Stay where you are,' Hackwood said. 'Let him get up if he can. Don't shame him.'

The girl halted. Her hand to her mouth, her eyes shining widely in the moonlit night, she watched Ned as he reached all-fours, then, slowly, lurching, regained his feet.

Then Hackwood moved forward again, on the balls of his feet and still a suggestion of a crouch in his bearing.

The girl cried, 'Stop it! Oh, stop it, both of you!'

Ned's hands moved up to cover himself. Hackwood's fists beat them aside, beat them down. He used his fists like blunt weapons, with thudding precision, calculated violence.

Teetering, Ned swung wildly, caught Hackwood on the temple, stopping him.

Hackwood shook his head as if something had stung him.

Ned launched himself foward and for a moment the two men, closing, were as one, a many-tentacled, threshing beast, raising the dust. Then they fell apart and Ned was teetering like a drunken man but backing instinctively,

4

his arms waving in front of him in a parody of defence.

And Hackwood followed him, his fists rising and falling and Ned groaned, a desperate sound, and the girl gave a thin scream.

Ned went to his knees and then slowly, all his joints giving way, he flopped forward on his face and lay still.

The girl went down on her knees in the dust beside him.

She looked up at Hackwood who stood, head bent and arms hanging, his lean chest rising and falling.

'You're just a savage!'

'You too, honey,' he said softly.

He went back to his horse and got his gunbelt and buckled it on.

He called softly, 'You better tell your Dad that Ned fell or somep'n... Take care of yourself. So long.'

She did not answer him.

CHAPTER TWO

Jasper and Fresco rode side by side.

Neither of them had spoken for a mile or so.

Then Fresco suddenly said: 'You should've been top-dog on that caper. Even though you was sick and dint take a big part, you set the

5

thing up, you planned it an' all, you should've had more, like.'

He still had a flavour of English about his speech, its idiom. With his parents he had immigrated to the States from the English North-country when he was a sprig. Nobody knew why he was called Fresco and whether it was his real name or not.

'Yeh,' said Jasper curtly. 'I guess I was outvoted.' Nobody called him anything else but 'Jasper'.

'You've allus bin a top man,' Fresco said. 'It ain't your fault you got sick. It could've been any of us after we passed through that bloody camp where folk were dying like bugs with that damn' fever or whatever it was. In any case, look at poor ol' Rube. He didn't get no fever. But he got himself gunned to death like a dog in the street during the job...' Fresco was younger and talked too much. The older man cut him short.

'Rube lived by killing and by taking chances. Just like the rest of us. We split his money, didn't we? You had some of it.'

'Yeh. We couldn't throw it away, could we?' Fresco sniggered. 'I even got a bigger cut than you this time, though by my reckoning that weren't fair.'

'I'm glad you told me that, son,' said Jasper sardonically. 'I'll let you buy me a drink in the next town.'

6

'Sure, pardner, as many as you like.'

It was a border town squatting near the waters of the Rio Grande with good grazing land nearby and a few metal mines in the hills.

Living was cheap down here, the food, the liquor, the women. A lawbreaker could easily ford the river to Mexico and lie low till whatever it was blew away with the hot breeze, as it always did. There was a lot of crime and not much law. And that suited loboes like Jasper and Fresco just fine.

The first thing the two men wanted was a drink. Jasper was a heavy drinker and Fresco went along with him, toe and toe on the brass rail, a bottle of rye and two glasses in front of them.

Fresco, who could not possibly match the tougher, older, partially-pickled Jasper soon began to show his liquor, became tearful and maudlin about his pard, Rube, 'shot down in his prime'. Rube had in fact been older than Fresco's present companion, Jasper, and he and Fresco had never been close—no more than Fresco and Jasper now, if it came to that, and if truth were told.

Rube had been getting stiff and slow and had got himself gunned down by a townsman when the bunch that had recently broken up had pulled their last express-office job.

Sick or well, Rube hadn't really been worth his *dinero*. Anyway, it was all dirt down a pipe

7

now as far as Jasper was concerned and he wished to hell that Fresco would quit jawing about it.

But Fresco continued to weep into his whisky, which maybe would make it taste a mite better, Jasper reflected: it was gunpowder and snake-head poison and no mistake.

Finally, Jasper, never the one to interfere with other folks, drunk or sober, merry or melancholy, said he aimed to look the town over.

'I'll be right with you, mate,' said Fresco. But as Jasper had already assumed Fresco, red hair sticking up on his head like a brush, was too unsteady on his pins to be going anyplace.

With Jasper's help, Fresco draped himself once more over the bar and Jasper asked the sick-looking half-breed barman if he had a room to let upstairs, a big one if possible.

The man said they could have the biggest of the lot. After a bit of dickering there was an exchange of some crumpled bills and Fresco who, head on one side, had been owlishly watching the two other men said:

'I guess I need some sleep. I guess it's been a hard day an' a hard trail. Yeh, I guess I'll go take myself a spot o' shut-eye.'

Even drunk he tended to run off at the mouth—even if he did have three goes at 'shut-eye' before getting it out intact.

When Jasper left the wide, dusty, sparsely-furnished room Fresco was lying snoring, still fully-clothed, on the outsized brass bed.

Jasper locked the door and pocketed the key.

He debated whether to leave Fresco where he was at and mosey on singly. Maybe he ought to throw the key away: he smiled thinly to himself.

But wild boy Fresco would probably shoot the lock off, or in some other way draw undue attention to himself. Jasper didn't want another posse on his tail because of a wild kid who couldn't hold his hooch. He decided he'd nurse Fresco for a while, maybe take him over the border, plant him there.

He got himself some food in a cantina and some tequila to go with it, followed by lashings of hot strong coffee.

He visited one or two other places, just for a look-see. He noted the location of various, and notable, establishments, including the marshal's office which was, as was customary, adjacent to the jailhouse.

He saw a few faces he knew—folks like himself.

Had they met on the trail they would have come together, exchanged yarns. But here they studiously ignored each other, or almost; a lifted eyebrow maybe, a nod, a quirk of the lips. Nothing more. Until, on the boardwalk a thin tall man stepped into Jasper's path.

'You got a light, suh?'

'Sure, friend.'

9

Jasper took out a box of lucifers, struck one and applied the flame to the drooping end of the man's hand-made cigarette.

'You never could roll worth a hoot, Nicky.'

The thin man grinned with broken teeth. Straggly hair like dirty straw escaped from beneath his battered felt hat.

'How've you bin, Jasper?'

'So-so.'

Jasper turned his head sideways to glance at Nicky's *compadre*, a long-moustachioed Mex called Santi who leaned indolently against a nearby hitching rack.

Nicky and Santi. They sounded like a cross-talk comedy-act but they were poison all through, certainly not the sort you'd mention in a letter to your sainted Maw.

Santi made a little gesture with one hand, but did not come any nearer. Jasper thought that both men, companion owlhooters from way back, looked kind of beat-down and frazzled round the edges.

'We saw you ride in earlier, Jasper,' said Nicky. 'You an' that new kid, the ginger one. Where'd you pick him up?'

'On the trail,' said Jasper laconically. 'Why, do you know him?'

'Nope. You onto something, Jasper?'

'Not particularly.'

Jasper sensed that Nicky, probably short of *dinero*, was fishing to see if his old saddle-pard,

10

Jasper, had something profitable in mind in which Santi and Nicky could join.

Santi and Nicky!

Like hell, thought Jasper. He told himself that he was way too smart now to be messing with stinking scum-bags like those two!

He had in fact spotted the two outlaws earlier when Fresco and he had ridden into town and he had pointed them out unobtrusively to the ginger-headed young man. Fresco had said he had heard of them, had even seen them once before, though he couldn't remember where.

'Be seein' you, Nicky,' said Jasper and walked around the thin man.

CHAPTER THREE

He finger-waved sardonically to Santi as he passed him.

The Mexican smiled thinly, the smile not reaching his moody black eyes. Jasper could feel those eyes boring into his back as he went on.

He wondered if somehow those two skunks had gotten wind of the recent express-office job. It hardly seemed likely.

He dismissed the two from his mind. They were no more to him than spit in the breeze.

He was accosted by two ladies of the town and politely turned down their coquettish invitations

11

to share in their fleshy experimentations.

He figured he might feel different later by night, a time to his way of thinking that was the best time of all for whooping and hollering and getting an edge on and the bit between the teeth and the old Adam rising and the partaking of the sins of the flesh.

Maybe he'd even find himself three of them then, even four! He grinned. In truth, after the food and a concoction of both North-American and Mexican booze on top of the long dusty ride he was beginning to feel a mite tired himself— maybe Fresco had had the right idea after all, if he could have been said to have any kind of idea at all in his wild head.

Jasper was feeling kind of itchy too, so he had a wash, complete with stinging yellow soap, at the pump in back of the saloon before he climbed the stairs.

Fresco was still snoring merrily, looking like a tow-headed kid blowing bubbles. Jasper rolled him off the bed and he came to rest with a thump on his side on the hard floor with its tattered rush mats. He curled up, cradling his cheek on his fist; he did not awaken. He stopped snoring though.

Jasper took one of the grimy pillows off the double-bed and rolled Fresco's head upon it. Fresco grunted something, then settled down again. He smelled like a well-fermented still in the middle of a swamp.

Jasper opened the window a crack, almost breaking his shoulder in the process. Cursing bitterly, fatigue and the hooch hitting him harder at last, he struggled out of his boots and took off his gunbelt and lay flat on his back on top of the bed. He kept his hat on, tilting this over his eyes.

He kept his gunbelt at his side. He lifted the hat again and stared owlishly at the door. Then he remembered he had locked it on the inside, leaving the key there. He got off the bed and padded across the room. Hell, he thought, my feet sure do stink! He took the key out of the lock, after testing to make sure that the door was actually locked, and put the key on the washstand by the window. Then he composed himself on the bed once more, tilted the hat forward, closed his eyes.

★   ★   ★

When Jasper awoke it was dark. He lit the lamp beside the bed. Fresco was no longer on the floor.

He was not even in the room, although he had closed the door behind him, unlocked, the key on the inside.

Jasper's gun, boots and everything else were just where he had put them. The only thing that Fresco had moved was the key, in order to let himself out. Even so, Jasper was savage with himself. He usually slept like a cat. He could not remember whether anything had disturbed him or not. Maybe Fresco had only just gone. The younker had certainly moved with stealth. Or maybe, Jasper thought, he himself had been more beat than he had realized.

He drew on his boots, buckled on his gunbelt. Sounds of growing activity filtered through the window to him and through the floorboards from the saloon below.

As he went down the stairs, the sounds from immediately below got louder, suddenly assuming an ugly tone which made the short hairs prickle at the base of Jasper's neck and his hand drop instinctively to his gunbelt.

The gunshots came with dramatic power, rolling up to him like thunder.

When he got to the bar-room everybody was looking at the batwings, which swung open, and Fresco came through. He was walking lopsided and his gun hung slackly, heavily in his fist at the end of his long arm. He was hatless and the lights made a halo of his red hair.

'Jasper,' he said. Then he fell flat on his face, his gun skittering along the floorboards. Jasper bent, picked it up and tucked it into his own belt.

There were two red-rimmed holes in Fresco's back, the red spreading, seeping. Down on one knee, his gun in his other hand, Jasper rolled Fresco over. He was half-looking at Fresco,

14

half-looking at the batwings, which were still now.

Fresco's eyes were open and wild. There was red froth around his lips. 'They got my *dinero*, Jasper,' he said. 'It was Nicky and Santi...'

His head fell back, hitting the boards with a small thump.

Jasper rose and moved to the side of the doors. He swung one heavily-booted foot and crashed one wing open. Nothing happened. Stooping low, crab-like, gun in hand, he went through.

He flattened himself against the wall in the shadows. People had heard the gunfire, were moving along the street towards the saloon. There was no Nicky, no Santi, no more shooting.

Jasper went back into the saloon. An oldster with shoulder-length grey hair was straightening up from Fresco. 'He's dead,' he said.

'Shore he's dead,' said Jasper. He holstered his gun slowly. His blue eyes stared at the old man, who shifted his feet nervously and asked, 'You his friend, mister?'

Jasper didn't answer the question; said, 'What happened?'

Three voices started up at once. Jasper pointed a finger at the old man. 'Let him tell it!'

The oldtimer said, 'He was playin' cards with them two fellers. A little Mexican with big moustachios and a long thin feller with hair like

15

straw. He was flashing money about like he'd just robbed a bank. He was drinking. Seemed like he was drunk already. Anyway—these two fellers got up . . . .'

Another voice chimed in, a weedy man with a yockety Adam's apple. 'I was right close. I heerd 'em say they'd gotta go down the street to tell some gels not to wait on 'em . . .'.

'They never seed no girls,' put in the long-haired oldtimer scornfully.

'Like I said,' went on Adam's Apple, with dignity. 'That's what I heerd 'em say, an' I heerd 'em say, too, that they'd be right back and the red-head should wait, an' he said he would.'

'They weren't long,' said the old man. 'They came back all right. An' that young jackass had his back to the door an' they both plugged him. One of them stripped him of his money while the other covered us. They were like lightning . . . But, Godamighty, that younker, he got up and he went after 'em; with the two holes in his back he went after 'em . . . .'

'Walkin' dead,' said Adam's Apple sententiously. 'Walkin' dead . . . .'

'Here's the marshal,' said somebody.

He was a paunchy man with a big moustache. Willing voices told him what had happened; there was no two ways about it. Then he turned to Jasper. 'You his pardner?'

'No,' lied Jasper. 'Just met him on the trail is all. Rode in with him. Seemed a nice young

16

feller. I'll pay for him to be buried though, Marshal. Least I can do.'

'That's white of you, stranger.' The lawman was impressed. Jasper thought him a bit stupid.

'Did anybody know the two men who did this?' the marshal wanted to know.

Nobody did it seemed. 'Two real hard nuts,' said Adam's Apple. He and the long-haired oldtimer had already given the lawman descriptions of Nicky and Santi.

'I didn't see 'em,' said Jasper. 'I was too late.'

'Do the descriptions mean anything to you?'

'No,' lied Jasper. He added, 'I was aiming to leave today. Got business up-country. Any objections, Marshal?'

'No, suh. You go ahead.'

'I'll go see the undertaker first. Least I can do.'

'Sure.'

Jasper looked down at the body and shook his head from side to side. 'He was a nice young feller. I think his name was Mart—or Martin, or somep'n like that. I shore hope them goddam killers get their come-uppance ere long.'

The undertaker appeared: a little dark-suited man with a white face and a huge nose which pulsated like a rabbit's at the smell of death. Jasper gave him some money and he was well pleased. The mortal remains of an English boy called Fresco were carted away. Jasper said he wouldn't stay for the funeral. Without asking

17

any direct questions he had learned which way the two killers had left town. They seemed to be going over the border as he had figured they would.

★   ★   ★

Nicky and Santi fooled him at first by back-tracking. They feared a posse (there had been one) but Jasper didn't imagine they knew he was on their trail or they might have tried a dry-gulch parlay.

It was a couple of weeks before he got a strong line on them and by then they were in Arizona, not far from the border but pushing inland away from the Rio all the time.

He was not far behind them, riding into a little one-horse burg just after they had left. After eating, washing-up and seeing to his horse he went on. It was night. From a bluff under the dark starless night he saw in the distance a light winking; it looked like a small campfire.

He pushed his horse on for a bit and then he halted again, seeing the patch of brightness bigger, knowing now for sure that it was a fire. He dismounted from the horse and took an old blanket from his saddlebag and tore it into strips. He bound the beast's hooves, talking to it gently as he did so. Then they went on more slowly, the horse stepping daintily, and now almost completely silent, the man erect in the saddle, limiting his own movements to the minimum.

The fire was bright through a few trees. Jasper left the horse, reins dangling, and he went forward.

They were hunkered at the small fire, drinking coffee. They both faced him. 'Hallo, boys,' he said.

They rose warily but, seeing that their visitor's hands were empty, they did not lower their own fingers to their guns, which they still wore; they hadn't yet got set for the night.

'Wal, howdy, Jasper,' said Nicky, his straw hair shining, red-tinged in the firelight.

Santi merely grunted a form of greeting. His guttural voice held no false welcome. Because of his black whiskers he looked the dirtier of the two.

Nicky said, 'Last time we saw you was in that li'l ol' town down on the border.'

There was still the false friendliness in his voice; he looked wary, his long form sloping. They're both pretty fast, Jasper thought. He wondered if they suspected anything. He didn't waste any more time. He said:

'Yeh, I saw you in that li'l ol' town. You saw a friend o' mine too. A ginger-headed young feller called Fresco. He had a hunk o' *dinero* with him. You grabbed it—after you shot him in the back.'

He saw the light in their eyes. He crouched.

19

His elbow pumped. The gun came out. An extension of his cupped hand. His arm shot out, the gun levelled like a rod. With his other hand, he fanned the hammer, moving the gun in a narrow half-circle.

Even as the two men crumpled, a slug flicked Jasper's shoulder.

Nicky had been knocked backwards; his legs kicked once and then he was still.

Santi swayed, dead on his feet, his hands empty. He fell on his face in the fire, bringing a spurt of flame and sparks.

Jasper searched the two bodies and took all the money he could find. The bag holding Santi's *dinero* was stitched to his belt. Jasper, the heat on his face, took his broad-bladed knife from its sheath and cut the bag free.

He moved off, went back to his horse, mounted up.

A little breeze rose and he thought he smelled burning flesh.

*   *   *

The fever came on him again very suddenly.

Maybe it was after the heat of the chase, the sourness of the killing.

He had no remorse though about killing two poisonous sidewinders like Nicky and Santi.

No, the bug must have still been lurking in his gut, dormant since the last time. And now,

20

because he was tired, frazzled, wanting to put himself as far away as he could from the express-office job, the killing of young Fresco, the killing of Fresco's murderers, it had flared up, started to bite again.

It was night and seemed to have gone cold. He managed to light a small fire and brew some coffee, even warm some beans. He managed to keep the coffee down—most of it leastways—but he spewed the beans up again.

What seemed like physical blows to his head, delivered with a huge mallet, were driving him down. His belly felt as if it were full of boiling acid.

He lay down beside the fire with his poncho over him and he tried to get warm.

He must have sort of passed out.

It could hardly have been called sleep . . . .

No man could sleep with all the devils of hell tormenting him to his very soul . . . .

CHAPTER FOUR

Hackwood was a lean, medium-sized man who had the strength and resilience and power of a well-oiled stockwhip. He was a handsome dark-haired man. There were lines cut in his lean cheeks, but his eyes were of a bright blue, his nose straight, his lips well-cut and with a humorous twist. He had a catlike, good-natured indolence about him that appealed to both sexes of the people he met. But, as he had demonstrated in the fight over the girl back at the ranch he had recently quit, he could be as ornery and violent as a wild cougar.

He had had a chequered career. He had been married once, to a red-headed Irish girl called Bridget. She had died suddenly during one wild winter in Kansas from a pestilence of the kind that often swept across the spaces of the bleaker western lands. The child she had been carrying at the time had died with her.

Hackwood's life had gone sour for a while after that. He sold out his small ranch and started an aimless sort of roaming. He shot a man and was caught and convicted. But there were mitigating circumstances and his sentence was not long.

He was not specifically owlhoot material, but he was a friend of owlhooters, an ex-jailbird, not a respectable small rancher anymore. He made his living in various ways and he did not stay in any one place overlong.

He liked ranchwork—in the early days it had been part of his life and his dreams—but he owed no loyalty to anyone or anything now and he came and went as he pleased.

He was moving along the border now, though for no particular reason, content to roam until he needed more cash, and then he would find means of getting it. He still had a fair amount of *dinero* left over from that last ranch job, as well as a few bruises to testify that he had not actually been showered with sweet-smelling flowers when he quit that particular go-round.

He paused briefly in a rough border-town where it seemed there had recently been a killing, although that was no rarity. A young man had been shot in the back by two other men who had lifted his stash. This blatant killing was still a desultory topic of conversation amid the heat and the flies.

Hackwood did not like the town or its people very much, so, after a bath—the iron tub was as grimy as the town—chow, coffee, a few drinks of rotgut that tasted like the drippings from a whore's washcloth, he moved on.

He was way, way out of the town—he had not even learned its name—and going away from the border when in the deep night he saw the flickering flame.

This was a flat, arid stretch of landscape and he had not seen a habitation for many miles.

He had not seen human or animal life for a long time either and he was wary now, slowing his horse to a steady walk as he approached the light, it getting brighter.

It was only a small fire though. And beside it lay a single, poncho-covered form.

Still Hackwood went warily, however. This could be some kind of trick, the poncho tucked

23

around a rolled blanket and men, guns drawn, waiting in the few trees—the first little clump for miles—as the unsuspecting pilgrim drew near.

Hackwood slid from the saddle and ground-hitched his pinto, a well-trained little beast, 'part-Injun' as the saying was, intelligent, tireless and fleet.

Hackwood did not draw his gun. There might indeed be a man in the poncho, and he alone, and maybe he was watching Hackwood approach and maybe he had a gun too, in the folds of his covering.

And a man approaching in the dark, gun in hand, warlike, might start a tired and disgruntled, *waking* pilgrim to a-blasting.

Hackwood moved on the balls of his feet, making a loop in his approach, a sort of small detour. He could have called 'Oh, the fire!' but he did not. He had once had a watch but he had lost it. He did not know what time it was now but he figured it was kind of late.

He was tired and saddlesore himself and it was time he hunkered down. He knew that if he had come upon this grove unoccupied this was where he would have stopped.

But, hell, there was room for more than one!

He saw that the fire was dying.

A horse was hitched to a tree and stood, head drooping. It looked as if it had been ridden half to death; but maybe it was just a lazy brute. It

24

had not in any way acknowledged the presence of another of its own kind, standing, waiting, but alert, nearby. And it did not even raise its head to look at the man in the darkness, the tiny flare of the fire picking out light on his belt-buckle and his spurs.

Hackwood was in the grove of trees by now and only a few yards from the tiny fire and the shrouded form beside it. If there were others in the spare trees they had little cover and he figured he would've spotted 'em. Hell, if there had been anybody there and they had had warlike intentions they could've blasted him to Kingdom Come by now!

'This is a friend,' he said softly.

The horse moved somnolently, raised its head a little, but then lowered it again. The form by the fire did not move at all and Hackwood went slowly nearer to it. Then he saw that it was shaking. Trembling maybe. Could a man be that scared? He reached it in two more strides, longer ones this time. He could not see a face.

He got down on one knee beside the shaking form and took hold of a fold of the poncho and drew it back and that was when the man rolled over.

Hackwood was so startled that his hand moved instinctively towards his gun, but he checked the motion. What he could see of the face in the fitful light from the dying flames of the fire held no menace for him.

25

The man made sounds. But they were not words. They were grunting, breathless complaints, formed in agony and half-delirium. This man was either sick or wounded and could not harm anyone. He was laid out like a pig for the slaughter, which was what would have happened to him—he would have been slaughtered and stripped—had some border scum happened onto him instead of Hackwood.

There was a canteen on the grass within reach of Hackwood's hand. He picked it up and shook it. It was empty. An empty tin cup lay on its side by the fire and there was a tin plate with stuff congealed upon it, looking like the residue of a mess of beans.

Hackwood rose and went back to his horse and got his own canteen.

'Godamighty,' he said as he got down again beside the only half-conscious form.

He knew that face!

The man took the water greedily, it dribbling down his chin.

'Take it easy,' said Hackwood, taking the receptacle away.

The man's eyes opened. They were bleary, hurt, puzzled. Then, slowly, they began to focus.

'Howdy, Jasper,' said Hackwood.

'Hack?' The voice was plaintive.

'Yes, it's me, Jasper.'

'Hell, Hack, I thought you was a mirage or

26

somep'n.' The man began to gasp with laughter; the sound dribbled out and his eyes closed again. But already his breathing was better.

★   ★   ★

Hackwood was able to ascertain that Jasper was not wounded but suffering from some kind of feverish sickness which made him alternately hot and cold, occasionally lucid and then like a mumbling crazy man.

Although Hackwood was kind of glad to see ol' Jasper again he hoped that what ailed the man, whatever it was, didn't happen to be catching. Two of 'em lying out here shaking like a couple of prairie dogs with the ague and as weak as two one-legged midgets in a cathouse was not a vision to contemplate. Although Hack had not seen any yet, there would be wild life in this territory, both animal and human. Hack didn't want Jasper and him to be skinned alive or nibbled to death.

Jasper was sleeping fairly peaceably now—so maybe the fever would soon break. Hack wrapped himself in one of his own raggedy blankets and propped himself against a tree with his gun in his lap.

He dozed fitfully.

He was not disturbed.

Jasper did not make much noise in his sleep.

And the dawn came, and then the sun began

to rise.

It was a goodish morning and a voice said, 'Where are you, Hack?' and Jasper rolled over to face him.

'Oh, there you are. You ain't a dream after all.'

'Nope, still large as life and better'n a bug on a hot griddle.'

'Yeh, you look fine.'

'Sorry I can't say the same for you, ol' pardner.'

'Yeh, I reckon I have been kinda porely. But I seem to be mendin'. I reckon I oughta thank you, Hack, wherever you sprung from.'

'Right now none o' that makes any nevermind....'

'You allus did talk kinda purty... Hell's Bells, Hack, my throat feels as if it's been scraped with a bunch o' cactus.'

Hack rose, stretching. 'I've got some water left,' he said.

CHAPTER FIVE

They had met in Yuma State Penitentiary when Hackwood had been serving his sentence for manslaughter.

They had shared a cell with an elderly small-time thief called Rapple, until Rapple had

28

suddenly died with peritonitis. He had not been replaced and Jasper and Hack had been a pair in the cell and had become firm friends.

Jasper was serving his sentence for a payroll robbery that had gone badly wrong. There had been three of them, and Jasper was the only surviving member of the trio. Armed guards had surprised them and gunned to death Jasper's two pardners.

Jasper had been lucky: he had merely got a knock on the head. He did not mourn his pards, he told Hack. They had just volunteered to help him on the caper and the one who had been supposed to check on the guards had done a bad job and had paid for that with his life. They had both been pretty stupid. So had he himself, Jasper said, lining himself up with such a pair of jackasses.

Jasper made Hack laugh, and, right then, he *needed* to laugh. Jasper had helped him to regain his own rather sardonic sense of humour.

In some ways they were two of a kind. There was not a lot of years between them, with Jasper being a little older; and they were both lean, fast men. Hack had more hair than Jasper and in jail Jasper had tried what he called 'scalp-massage'; but had not helped his follicles none, and now propped up at the fireside where Hack had coaxed out flames again and, without the hat he invariably wore except while sleeping Jasper looked like a monk with a bushy black tonsure.

Anyway, he was uglier than Hack, if quite pleasantly so. Neither of them looked particularly lethal, though Jasper undoubtedly was. . . .

Hack had left Yuma Pen before his friend had, but they had promised to catch up with each other.

Hack had got a job on a ranch and, after being released himself, Jasper had joined his old cell-mate there for a while: the boss didn't object to ex-cons as long as they worked pretty well: he only paid chickenfeed anyway.

But Jasper was no ranny and he eventually lit out.

Hack promised to catch up with him later. But he never had.

Not until last night by the fireside.

He would not have been surprised if he had found Jasper with a bullet in him. Neither of them had changed a hell of a lot, though Jasper of course still looked kind of sick. But Hack had a feeling that a lot of water had passed under the bridge and not all of it had been clean.

Hell, in jail or out he had never had any illusions about Jasper. And, come to think of it, his own career since leaving the pen had not exactly been unsullied white all over all the time.

It was two days later and they were riding side by side.

Jasper was almost good as new again,

beginning to look like his old self when he asked, not for the first time, 'Well, are you with me then, Hack, old pard?'

And Hack, not even hesitating now, said:

'Yeh, I'm with you, Jasper.'

And those two sentences were the start—if not to put too fine a point on it—of a chain of events, the links of which were to touch more than a few lives and to make Jasper and Hack notorious, if comparatively unsung; and not exactly heroes.

★   ★   ★

The first link of the chain was forged when two lean men with generous-sized coloured bandannas over their faces and slouch hats pulled down so that only their shaded dark eyes could be seen held up a stage office and got away with a sizeable bundle of pay-roll money— mainly for nearby silver mines—which had only recently been delivered, and the extra contingent of armed guards just left to boot.

The two remaining stand-by guards were disarmed without even the smallest speck of blood being spilled and, with the cold barrel of a .44 Colt pressed to the back of his neck the clerk was persuaded to open the huge steel safe.

Although it was through a job of this kind that Jasper had been sent to jail he still maintained that, if you did your groundwork

31

first and then played your cards cool they were usually easier than banks or railroads.

Hack was inclined to agree with him—and there wasn't so much danger of innocent bystanders getting hurt either, though Jasper hadn't bothered to mention that particular fact.

They rode hard afterwards, for they knew there was bound to be a posse on their tail sooner or later: the mine authorities certainly wouldn't sit still for this lot.

'Fat bastards back East drinking vintage wines,' Jasper said. 'This'll hurt their goddam pride as well as their goddam profits. Hell, Hack, it ain't criminal to steal from fat, rich pigs like that. They'll have to fix another payroll an' the miners 'ull get paid in a few days—they ain't losing much by this.'

'I heard there was some ranchers' money as well among that,' said Hack.

'That's their bad luck,' said Jasper sourly. 'Teach 'em to get their *dinero* through some other way in future 'stead o' mixing it with money belonging to fat Eastern bastards and that's squeezed from the blood an' sweat o' pore souls labouring underground like tormented mortals in Hell.'

'Who's talking purty now then?' said Hack. 'My, my, but you do go on!'

Hack had more than a sneaking suspicion that in reality Jasper had no social conscience at all, if it could be called that. He had an idea that

Jasper cared no more for miners than he did for anybody else who was jackass enough to earn his bread by honest toil. He was a bigger and more ruthless brigand than any fat cat back East, if a more straightforward one.

To think of Jasper as 'straightforward' was a bit of a jest. But he had been very straightforward with his saddle-pard, Hack; and now it seemed he was trying to build up Hack as some kind of Lincoln Green 'goodheart' to go with his own Western-style Robin Hood.

Maybe this was a sort of conscience-saver. Not a conscience-saver for Jasper himself, who had been on the owlhoot since he was a boy, but a conscience-saver for Hack, who was a comparative 'new boy'.

'Quit all the fancy jawing, Jasper,' Hack said. 'That's supposed to be my line of country, remember. We got the *dinero* didn't we?'

Jasper had told Hack about the earlier raid when, about that time he had had his first bout of sickness. He had told him about the murder of young Fresco and the vengeance that he, Jasper, had exacted from the two men who had gunned-down the lad.

Hack knew that Jasper was a killer. He himself had so far only killed one man and for that he had been put in Yuma Jail where he, of course, first met Jasper.

He had told Jasper about the girl back at the ranch—her name had been Allie—and the fight with the young man called Ned, who was the man chosen by her father to be her bridegroom. He had also been the ranch foreman so that was a sweet deal all round. But, while Hack was at the spread Allie had preferred to spend her evenings in the barn with him rather than on the porch swing with her betrothed.

'Hell, Hack,' said Jasper. 'One of these days you're gonna be dragged to Perdition by your own goddam tail.'

He laughed.

Hack said: 'Jasper, old hoss, there sure as hell are worse ways to go.'

They had a sizeable haul now, including the money that Jasper had culled from his previous job and which he insisted, despite Hack's protests, should be thrown in the pot with the rest.

'You have young Fresco's share,' he said. 'He ain't likely to need it where he's gone.'

They had not seen any signs of a posse and figured that if there was one—and there was certainly likely to be—they were well ahead of it now.

Maybe the posse had a good tracker with it. But Jasper thought he had outfoxed whoever that might be. The lean sparse-haired man was not particularly old in years but he was certainly old in trail-craft. He knew more tricks than a card-sharp with a doctored deck, a derringer in his armpit and a stiletto in his boot.

34

Come to think of it, Jasper was a pretty tricky customer all round. And, although he didn't keep a little sneak cannon in a shoulder-holster or a knife in a low-down hideout he was, all in all, pretty well armed.

He had two guns, one kept in a conventional side holster, the other in the front of his belt in a sort of sling made up of an old bandanna. He kept a knife in a pouch on his belt too, on the opposite side to his gun-sheath and he had a jack-knife he kept in his pocket and that he used for cutting plug-tobacco but which would make a formidable weapon also.

He had a Winchester in a saddle-scabbard, which matched Hack's own long gun. Hack had a big-barrelled Navy gun in his holster on the right hip but no back-up gun; and his knife was a itsy-bitsy thing which he used for small chores and wouldn't carve anything tougher than cheese.

In Texas now, they were moving further away from the border all the time.

Just two saddle-tramps. Looking for work maybe.

On their last job they had been well-masked.

Hack had to admit that, with careful planning, the caper had been just as simple as Jasper had said it would be.

And who could catch up with them now; who would recognize them?

They passed herds of longhorns, ranches,

smallholdings; big-hatted cowboys waved to them from time to time.

They stopped in small cowtowns for eats and drinks but they slept on the trail. You were not noticed so much if you slept on the trail: that was what Jasper said, and so far he seemed to be talking turkey.

They forded creeks and once a river, though they did not know which river it was. Jasper went by landmarks rather than by names, and now he was beginning to run out of landmarks. They passed smallholdings and once a horse ranch and even a small pig-farm. While on high ground they saw in a valley below an old-fashioned wagon train winding its way sedately along.

'This is good ranching country, Jasper,' Hack said.

'Yeh, if you'd like to break your back.'

★   ★   ★

They lighted down eventually in a middling-sized cowtown called Mainsville because Hack said he wanted a bath and a real bed.

'You ain't dirty,' said Jasper.

'I am,' Hack told him. 'I stink! And so do you.'

'Well, thank you for tellin' me.'

'That's all right.'

Anyway, Jasper accompanied Hack to the

bath-house which, as was often the way, was in back of the barber-shop. They had shaves too, and haircuts with pomade, and Jasper said it was time he got a new hat.

They finished up by buying complete new outfits, though not new armoury. Anyway, soon they hardly looked the same two men who had ridden into town in the late afternoon.

Jasper said: 'Hell, Hack, nobody's gonna recognize us now.'

'I guess you're right, Jasper.'

'On the other hand,' said Jasper, musingly. 'There is something a bit distinctive about you.'

'I hope you mean that as a compliment, bucko.'

'Oh, sure, sure. But I ain't exac'ly talkin' about you, I'm talkin' about your horse. That pinto with all them paint-patches is certainly distinctive and somebody might have spotted him.'

'I hadn't thought o' that.'

'No, well... Now, my ol' mule-head, there's plenty of other nags look like him, ugly-lookin' bastard that he is. But your paint....'

'I'm kind of attached to that paint.'

'Yeh, I kin understand that, pard. A man gets that way about a horse, particularly if he's a good 'un, and that paint's a good 'un. He's fast and he's intelligent.'

'Too true.'

'And so is ol' mule-head, ugly or not!'

'I ain't saying he ain't. You trying to start an argument or somep'n. What've you got against my paint?'

'Nothing. He's a dandy horse. But, like I said, he's sort of, kind of—er—distinctive.'

'So he's distinctive,' snorted Hack. 'Whadyuh want me to do, buy a can o' black goo an' paint him all over?'

'Oh, by Jupiter!' cried Jasper. *'Fergit it!'*

CHAPTER SIX

The bulk of the payroll money snatched by Jasper and Hack had belonged to the Apex Silver Mine and the troubleshooter for them was a middle-aged walrus-moustached individual named Pete Ricken. Though not as young as he used to be he still had a good rep which he had earned as a lawman, mainly in the border areas, before moving on to the more lucrative profession of troubleshooting, first for a stage-line and then for Apex.

The payroll guards had left prematurely from the stage-office, not waiting for the arrival of the contingent from the mine, or even for one or two of the small ranchers whose *dinero* was there too.

The mine contingent was being led by Pete Ricken and they were held up, though not by anything human. And they did not learn till later that it was by human agency. The leaning tree had been beside the trail a long time and was a familiar landmark. Nobody had ever thought it would actually fall.

It lay across the trail that morning, however, and with its long, stout twisted branches blocked it completely. And the canyon walls loomed steeply each side of it: even if a man climbed them he could not get his horse by. So the party had to make a detour; and it was a wide one.

And by the time the party got to their destination the robbers and the payroll were long gone.

Subsequent investigation proved that the old leaning tree—and it had been leaning further in recent years—had been given a push. And more. In that the thick rubbery roots, exposed for so long yet still holding, had been severed completely by powerful blows of an axe. The weight of the old tree with its wide-stretching branches and its heavy foliage had torn the tap-roots out cruelly, showing them jaggedly-white, and the ancient monster had crashed, blocking the canyon enormously from wall to wall.

But, if only the other guards had stayed back at the base, instead of leaving only the two locals, both of them kind of long in the tooth; and the young clerk, not a gun-toter, just a penpusher!

Pete Ricken ranted and raved, but that did no good. And the walrus-moustached old lawman, knowing his bosses, and the faceless hawks back East who controlled them, realized that he was going to get most of the blame for all this.

The two robbers had been well-masked and behatted. Descriptions of them were sketchy, and pretty useless. Lean; medium height; youngish; darkish. Only one of them had spoken—he had seemed a mite older than the other one. His instructions had been terse and guttural and he had handled himself like a pro.

At the office the two men had left nothing behind. No clues at all.

Pete Ricken ranged the town, hoping to meet somebody who had seen the masked men ride out and could give a better description.

One thirteen-year-old-kid, who had been near the office when the men came out, had spotted something. No, not about the men, about one of the horses.

When the kid got near the office the horses had been outside.

And one of 'em was a lovely little pinto.

The kid just purely loved horses.

He described that pinto to Pete Ricken as if he, the kid, had sat there and painted it on canvas. . . .

He had seen the masked men come out of the office, still with guns in their hands, and he had frozen. They had looked about them and he figured that both of them had spotted him. But neither of them had spoken, or had menaced him in any way.

They looked like the people in the office had described them—the kid couldn't go any further than that.

The second horse? Cripes, that had just been a jughead—though pretty fast, the kid reckoned.

But that pinto had moved smooth as cream. . . .

If I'd had a gun I could've shot those two bandits, the kid boasted. And then I could've had that pinto for my own.

Maybe, said Pete Ricken, maybe.

He wondered if he could find a pinto like that one. . . .

★   ★   ★

A pinto, from the Spanish 'paint', is a piebald horse. They come in all sizes. The Indians and the cowboys loved the smaller, faster ones, the cayuses or cow-ponies. Every remuda tried to have at least one pinto and any cowboy who owned one of these distinctively-marked (though the marks varied) beasts was a proud man indeed. And any Indian who could capture, win or steal one had something that was worth more than three wives if his particular tribe stood for that sort of thing.

Hackwood had won his pinto in a poker-game and, to soften the blow a bit had given its disgruntled owner his, Hack's, own horse in sort of part-exchange.

The pinto was a small but exceedingly well built stallion. The gink from whom Hack won the beast had not, as far as Hack knew, given the pinto a name. The pinto did not seem to need a name. Sometimes Hack called him 'beauty', sometimes 'oldtimer', sometimes 'boy', sometimes 'little pardner'. The horse responded to the tone of the man's deep voice, though sometimes with a quizzical sidelong look that seemed to say 'what do you think I am, stupid or something'? And stupid he certainly was not.

Once in the early days the horse had tried to bite his rider, maybe just to test what kind of stuff this new man was made of. Hack punched him in the nose and called him an 'ornery little son-of-a-bitch'. This seemed to put the relationship on an understandable footing and man and horse had been good prairie-mates ever since.

Hackwood's pinto had huge splashes of chocolate-brown on a white field, with a distinctive pear-shaped mark big as a man's fist on his left flank and a long mark like a large tear running from his left eye down to his nose.

And this was the pinto that Pete Ricken, gunfighter and troubleshooter, walrus-moustached, cantankerous, indomitable, was looking for.

★   ★   ★

Looking like a pair of dudes but, for safety's sake, still toting their well-worn hardware, Jasper and Hack sought a good place to eat.

The local barber, who doubled as bath-attendant, had told them the best chow to be had in Mainsville was at the hotel.

Mainsville had only one hotel and as it was bang in the centre of town it was not hard to find. It was a clean, newly-painted and quite imposing place, even though its false front soared way above its second storey.

There was a desk and a clerk with a white boiled front—the clerk not the desk—and a wide staircase and double doors to the left with the inscription DINING ROOM lettered above them. And Jasper and Hack turned sharply left and then marched ahead.

The desk clerk called, 'Can I help. . .?'

But the two men had gone, the double doors swinging gently behind them. The desk clerk, though still young, was as much a student of human nature as your average mossybacked range cook, who probably knows more about human nature than any other body in the whole South-west. He had thought at first that those two ginks were ranchers. They looked too prosperous to be merely cowhands. But there was something about the way they carried themselves, the way they walked. . . .

And those guns. The way they toted them! Particularly the older one, who looked as if he was going bald. He had a low-slung shooter at his hip, almost on his thigh really, and another one in the front of his belt.

Hardhats, thought the young man, and wondered whether he should pop down the street and tell the marshal.

No sweat, he thought though; those two aren't doing any harm; who in hell would want to stick up a dining-hall?

Maybe they had heard how good Missy Prentiss's pancakes were and aimed to steal themselves a stack.

The clerk grinned to himself and started to chew his nails. Hell, he was bored!

Hackwood would have been surprised had he learned the clerk's assessment of him as a hardhat, a hardcase. Yes, Jasper had that stamp on him all right. But Hack, if he had thought about it, would have opined that *he* didn't have that stamp yet—and that maybe he never would.

He had decided that he wanted another ranch some day, even if he began small the way he had done before. And working with Jasper was the quickest way to start getting this.

And Jasper certainly wasn't getting any

younger; surely he would want to settle down sooner or later: no gun-toter could go on forever. . . .

The old sadness was leaving Hackwood. He seldom thought now of his late wife and the son (or maybe the daughter) that might have been and the life they could have shared together. Part of the credit for this merciful forgetting must go to Jasper, and Hack would never forget his old cellmate and saddle-pard for that. If there was anything he could ever do for ol' Jasper. . . .

What Hack was actually thinking about when, with Jasper at his side, he entered the dining-room of the hotel in Mainsville was debatable. Maybe he was just thinking of food.

But when he saw the tall, beautiful redhead who was waiting on the tables all he could do was look at her, think about *her*.

CHAPTER SEVEN

The dining-hall was high and spacious and full of chairs and tables and white linen and crockery. There was a warm smell of good food. Many of the tables were already occupied and there was a bustle, a buzz, a cheerful clatter.

The redhead was moving among the tables, serving. Hackwood heard somebody call her

45

'Missy'. She was tall and she moved lithely and even the wrap-around apron she wore—it was colourful, Indianlike—did little to conceal her superb shape. She was about twenty and her features were beautiful. 'Classical' Hack would have called them: he had done some schooling, read some books. Her hair was not carroty, it was a full, flaming red; abundant, wavy.

Jasper and Hack found themselves an empty table and were accosted by a small, dumpy girl with pad at ready. Hack was disappointed—particularly as the girl called Missy disappeared into the kitchen. They learned later that she ran the dining-rooms and did most of the cooking herself, only serving on table at busy periods.

The barber had not steered them wrong. Redheaded Missy was a fine cook.

They had pot roast with sultanas and gravy and on the side boiled and roast potatoes, cabbage with herbs and young carrots. There were green peas in a deep dish and a mixed salad, fresh and sweet, of the like neither of them had seen in years.

The soup had been a mixed vegetable: obviously Missy had a good supplier for her greenstuffs, which were not enormously plentiful in the dry places of the West and thus expensive.

And right now the boys had deep-dish apple pie with dates and cheese and then coffee, and there was brandy if they wanted it. They had brandy.

'Golly Moses,' said Jasper. 'This is a bit of a change from tinned pork 'n' beans ain't it?'

'Shore is.'

They got cigars from the dumpy waitress and they lit up. They leaned back expansively in their chairs and blew smoke rings at the ceiling.

'This is the life,' said Jasper.

And Hack was inclined to agree with him.

Hack had watched the dumpy waitress as she moved away. She had a fascinating wiggle on her. Like two fat rats gambolling in loosely-packed sacks of meal. But, although the girl had given him the high sign, he couldn't really work up much enthusiasm.

He wanted to see Missy again.

People were moving out of the dining-rooms, their bellies and their souls replenished, going back to their daily tasks. The place was becoming empty.

And at last Hack's patience was rewarded. Missy came out to help clear tables.

And that was when the two gamblers came in.

At least, they looked like gamblers. They were not plump enough for drummers and did not smile enough.

They did not smile at all.

They were silent and they moved without effort.

Gamblers do not usually come in pairs, but maybe these two had a new system working with which to fleece the suckers.

They both wore black broadcloth and sported the obligatory fancy vest. They wore string ties. They both had their hats off and were carrying them in their hands. They were fine-looking, black broad-brimmed hats.

Their boots were almost knee-high, and highly-polished. They had high heels. Good riding boots. No spurs. Maybe they had left them with their horses. They both wore gun-rigs.

His gun-rig: that was what often gave a man away.

Although Jasper and Hack did not know it, their gun-rigs had given them away to the desk-clerk in the lobby, new clothes or no new clothes. And undoubtedly that young gink had had a good look-see at these two new arrivals and drawn his own conclusions, as Jasper and Hack now did.

The clothes that the two new arrivals wore were fine and dandy, looked pretty new. But their gun-rigs certainly were not new, though they were fine and dandy too, slung low, polished and oiled, obviously well-cared for.

These two characters with their low-slung guns both shot Jasper and Hack sharp but cursory glances and, then, sitting at an empty table, gave their full attention to the menu.

And, in this neck of the woods, how many establishments of this kind had a menu?

The dumpy waitress had just gone into the kitchen with a loaded tray of dirty crockery, so it was Missy who approached the two men, taking her order pad from the voluminous pocket of her apron and with it a stub of pencil.

The two men, though at first glance much of a muchness and of about the same height and age and build (give or take a few years they were of Jasper and Hack's generation) differed considerably in their features.

And in this they matched Jasper and Hack too: the handsome, the not-so-handsome.

The smooth-faced one, and there was a smooth-faced one, had a profile like a Greek God. His companion had a black moustache and bushy sideburns that hid a lot of his face, but not his fleshy, hooked nose and his small squint eyes.

Both men turned appreciatively towards the red-headed Missy, as well they might.

The handsome one gravely inclined his head and showed his beautiful double row of white teeth.

'Good morning, miss,' he said.

It was, actually, afternoon and these two looked like being the last customers in the dining-hall.

But the girl said: 'Good morning, gentlemen,' in a sweet, husky voice, and:

'I await your pleasure.'

The look of her was seductive. Or maybe it

was the words that did it. Maybe one of the two men at least had imbibed too freely elsewhere before entering the dining-hall—for, apart from adjacent saloons, the hotel had a bar too.

It was the ugly one who laid his hand on her.

And Jasper and Hack both saw it and both half-rose.

Missy slapped the man's face.

It was a round-house blow with the open palm and the sound of it was like a rifle-shot. It rocked the man back in his chair.

The legs of the chair came down with a thump and, cursing, the ugly man lurched to his feet. What he did next was purely a reflex action—as his hand moved down to the butt of his gun.

Then both Jasper and Hack were all the way up and their right hands were full of iron and Jasper called, 'Hold it there, both of you.'

'Sit down, pig!' said Hack.

Maybe the ugly cuss had been called 'pig' before. He sat down. His handsome companion turned his head to look at the two interlopers, but the rest of him did not move at all.

Missy backed away, over to the side, giving the two men with guns an even clearer view of their might-be targets than they had had before.

'Put your empty hands on top of the table,' Jasper told them, and they did that.

And Hack said out of the corner of his mouth, 'Keep the pretty one away from me while I teach his friend a lesson.'

50

'Be my guest, pardner ... Raise those hands from the table now, muh buckoes, an' push 'em way up into the air.'

The pair, whether they were gamblers or not, knew a stacked deck when they saw one. They raised their paws carefully until they were upstretched to their full length.

'Now get up from the table and back away from it.'

The ugly one, already on his feet, made this with alacrity. But his companion, seated, hands in air was a mite off-balance.

But he was not as clumsy as he pretended to be. He reached for the table to steady himself and Jasper let him get away with that ...

But when the handsome cuss straightened he had his gun in his hand, lifting.

He was mighty fast.

But he had been kind of foolish also.

Jasper shot him in the wrist.

His gun hit the floor, skidded across it and came to rest well away from either of the two men. The handsome one fell back into his chair, pushing it away from the table. His face white, he sat and clutched his wrist. Blood dripped to the floor.

The ugly man had also moved back from the table, in the opposite direction to his friend. He kept his hands in the air, and, after one glance at his bleeding friend, levelled his eyes at Jasper and Hack.

'That was some shooting, old hoss,' said Hack.

'I can do it again if anybody needs it,' Jasper said.

He levelled the gun at the ugly one.

Hack put his own gun back in its holster. He began to walk slowly towards the ugly one.

The girl, Missy, stood still, only her eyes shifting. They were wide and startled and her face looked strained.

'That's enough,' she said. 'Please.'

'I guess it will have to be though,' said Hack. 'Sometime.'

'Not here then.'

'All right.' Hack came to a halt.

Jasper barked. 'You—pig! Better get your friend to a doctor. Move!'

Slowly, the ugly man lowered his hands. But he kept them away from his sides, well away from his gun or any other weapon he may have had stashed out of sight.

He skirted the table and joined his friend, said, 'Come on.'

They went out side by side, the handsome one leaving a trail of bloodspots behind him.

The young desk clerk came through the door after the two men had disappeared. Both Jasper and Hack had put their guns away but the clerk, though he looked a mite scared had a forty-five in his fist.

'It's all right, Jimmy,' said the girl quickly.

52

'If you say so, Missy.' The boy withdrew.

But his place was taken a few moments later by an elderly grey-haired gent with a star on his breast.

CHAPTER EIGHT

Walrus-moustached troubleshooter Pete Ricken had with him his own sidekick, young Bob Bendix, a Wells Fargo man named Perrier, and a half-Apache half-Dutch tracker called Toledo.

So far it had been a fairly frustrating journey, entailing a lot of sniffing around and muttering and doubling-back by Toledo.

The half-breed was the best there was and, despite the snide remarks of Perrier, who obviously didn't like any kind of Indian, Pete went along with Toledo all the way. Even so the ex-lawman was still chawing himself alive with impatience.

Young Bendix, who was not over-bright but dead reliable, was his usual taciturn self, almost as taciturn as Toledo who only emitted a short string of unintelligible grunts from time to time. They weren't Apache, though Perrier obviously thought they were and was unaccountable irritated by them. They weren't Anglo either; they weren't anything in particular.

When Toledo was drunk, which was most of

53

the time when he wasn't working, he was known to dance and sing and talk a blue streak. He spouted quite decent Anglo too. But when he was working—and tracking was about all he knew—he seemed to only talk to himself. Nobody else understood his gruntings anyway.

On this trip, Toledo was emitting quite a lot of gruntings and eventually Pete Ricken got the drift: the men they were following, or one of them anyway, was an expert on the trail and was covering his traces pretty well.

That makes at least three pros on this job anyway, thought Pete sardonically: that other feller, and Toledo, and Pete himself. Young Bob Bendix was just a learner, and a pretty slow one at that. And, as for Wells Fargo man, Perrier, Pete wasn't sure what he was.

Perrier, who was thirtyish and long and lugubrious-looking, did more than his fair share of gabbing, which was pretty easy after all with two close-mouthed individuals like Toledo and Bob. And Pete Ricken himself, who was old enough not to want to waste energy, only talked when he figured he had something worthwhile to say—which wasn't often so far on this trip!

But Perrier seemed to be talking all the time, complaining, sneering, bragging. Obviously, as a member of a nationwide and famous organization and caught up with these far-Western peasants through no fault of his own, he figured he was hell in boots. . . .

54

I hope to hell that, if the time happens along, that braying jackass can fight as hard as he flaps his gums, thought Pete sourly. Perrier wasn't impressing anybody, not even good-natured Bob Bendix who was now at the point when he kept giving the Wells Fargo man puzzled glances.

It was getting dusk, and Perrier moaned, 'We can't go on forever, it's time we rested.'

Toledo made a few grunting sounds and pointed ahead.

Pete Ricken managed to get the gist of this, or thought he had. He said to Perrier, 'Toledo think there's a town ahead.'

But Toledo didn't think, he knew. . . .

But he didn't know what he was walking into; none of them did.

★   ★   ★

The grey-haired marshal of Mainsville was named Jack Muldoon and he was a friend of Missy's.

Missy's dad had, in fact, been Jack's best friend and also Mainsville's first mayor, and the longest-standing. He was still mayor when he was gored to death by a runaway mad bull on the trail outside town. He was out walking alone at the time, 'worry-walks' he had called them; and he the most unworrying of men!

His wife had died many years before when

their only daughter, Missela, was only eight years old.

'Missy', as she had become, missed her father greatly; and so did the town. And so did Marshal Jack Muldoon.

He was a bachelor and a loner. He had been a lawman for most of his adult life and that tended to make a man something of a loner, unless he went off politicking as many lawmen more famous than Jack had done. Jack wasn't the type though!

Jack had never taken kickbacks from gamblers or madams or saloon keepers.

He had never set himself up to be a noted *pistolero*, although he was pretty good with a gun if he had to be. He had killed men, but only in the line of duty.

Mainsville suited him fine and he aimed to stay there until he retired to a rocking-chair or they had to shovel him into the ground. On the whole Mainsville was a prosperous town; peaceable too, though much of that was due to Jack's own continued efforts.

Nowadays, although he kept his well-worn Frontier-model Colt in good trim he seldom took it out of its holster in any threatening way.

When he walked into the dining-hall of the Mainsville hotel that afternoon and confronted Missy and the two strangers his gun was still in its holster. He was a brave and forthright man.

He levelled brief, hard glances at the two

56

men. Then he said:

'You all right, Missy?'

'Yes, Jack, thank you.'

'What happened?'

Apart from the trio now confronted by Jack there were two other people in the dining-hall, a local married couple named Brent who ran a nearby dry goods store. They bustled forward now and, from one and the other—all five people putting in a two cents worth each now— the marshal got the story.

And Jasper and Hack, to their secret amusement, came up smelling sweeter than roses.

Jack Muldoon said: 'The doc will see to that jasper who got shot. . . .'

'Not this Jasper,' chuckled Hackwood, with a jerk of his thumb.

'No, not that Jasper. I gotta commend you boys.'

'Wasn't nothing, Marshal,' said Jasper. 'Those boys were well outa line. The ugly one anyway, though he ain't the one who got shot.'

'And I wouldn't trust the pretty one, perforated or not, any further than I could kick him,' said Hack.

'Like I was gonna say,' went on the marshal. 'I better check on that wounded one anyway— and make sure the two of 'em ain't got something else in mind, like revenge for instance.' He turned to the girl. 'You want to

57

charge either o' those two with anything, Missy? . . .

'I could stick him in the cooler and let him kick his heels for a bit.'

'No, Jack, let it be, please.'

'Just as you say, Missy . . . And thank you-all, gents.'

Jack Muldoon took his leave, and so did the Brent couple, who had to get back to business. Missy turned to the two strangers, who had effectively introduced themselves.

'Will you take a drink with me, gentlemen?' she said.

They went into the bar and sat at a corner table. Many people had gone back about their business. The topic of conversation—the recent un-fatal shooting—had been worried quickly to death. If you hadn't actually witnessed the incident there wasn't much to talk about anyway.

Now customers were thinner on the ground and talk was desultory. A fat white-aproned man came over to the corner table, his big, red face splitting in a giant-size grin.

'You all right, Missy?'

'Fine, thanks, Beany. Give my two friends what they want. And I'll have my usual.'

Beany turned his beaming attention to the two men. 'I've got a modicum of fine bourbon, gents. There ain't much of it around these parts.'

58

'Bourbon 'ull do me fine,' said Jasper.

'Me too,' said Hack.

★   ★   ★

Later, as the two of them sat on a bench near Mainsville's somewhat apologetic sort of square Hack said:

'It'd do no harm for us to stay here for a while, rest up sort of.'

Jasper chuckled. 'Hell, pardner, maybe the girl's married.'

Hack laughed. 'That one. I don't think so. Anyway, who said anything about the girl?'

Jasper did not bother to answer the question, dismissing it as irrelevant. He said:

'Come to think of it though, this might make a good base for operations, providing we don't mess too near our own doorstep, if you see what I mean.'

'I see what you mean,' said Hack, a bit doubtfully.

Jasper went on: 'After all, we have made a good starting impression, have been welcomed into the bosom of the town, so to speak.'

Hack said: 'You're allus on the lookout for the main chance ain't you?'

'The main chance is what counts in this business,' said Jasper, and Hackwood knew what business his partner meant.

And Jasper continued: 'I hadn't thought

about it before, I was quite prepared to ride on—but you started me thinking. I ain't come across that marshal before and I don't figure he knows me. I don't think there're any dodgers out for me either. And that marshal seems a good-natured ol' duck.'

'Good-natured, yeh—but tough. Don't sell him short.'

'I ain't aiming to... Anyway, let's give it a few days, huh, a few decent cracks of the whip?'

'Sure, sure, that's what I meant in the first place.'

'We'll have to find someplace to stay then.'

'They'll probably have room in the hotel.'

'That's what I thought you'd say.'

'Maybe we should've asked.'

'But we weren't thinking about it then were we? Leastways, I wasn't. Were you?'

'It did cross my mind.'

'I'll bet!' Jasper chuckled dirtily. 'I'll bet other things crossed your mind as well.'

They rose to their feet and crossed the 'square', walking awkwardly on baked, uneven ground in their high-heeled half-boots.

CHAPTER NINE

It was almost dark when troubleshooter Pete Ricken led his party into the little town which

60

wasn't much more than a dried-up mudhole in the prairie.

Lights were coming on and they made for the brightest of these.

They were a somewhat ill-assorted quartet.

The hard-bitten, walrus-moustached Pete looked just what he was, a man who lived by the law and by the gun. He gave the same kind of loyalty to his present employers, the mine-owners, that he had given to his badge and his town when he had been a law-officer.

His sidekick, Bob Bendix, did not look much like a troubleshooter, more like a slow-thinking waddy, which was what he had been before he had put in for a job with the mining organization. Bob was healthy and loyal and reliable. He always did what he was told. So maybe, in the long run he was a better choice where Pete Rickens was concerned than some quicker-witted but gun-happy younker.

Toledo? Well, Toldeo was Toledo. Phlegmatically Dutch. Inscrutably Indian. When he wanted to be that is. But the finest tracker Pete had ever known, and a loyal friend.

If there was any fly in the ointment as far as Pete was concerned it was the Wells Fargo man, Perrier. A long, lugubrious moaning son-of-a-bitch who was beginning to give mossyhorn Pete a nagging pain in his rawboned butt.

All Pete wanted to do was shove Perrier onto a cot someplace and let him sleep the way he kept complaining he wanted to. Then maybe he would quit his jawing, unless he talked in his sleep, and Pete wouldn't have been surprised at that—or maybe he snored and whistled and blew bubbles! Thank God I've still got a sense of humour, Pete thought, or I'd be kicking that one's ass plumb back to where he came from. . . .

The brighter lights turned out to belong to a large, if gimcrack, wood and 'dobe drinking establishment.

Everybody, even including Perrier, said that, storm on storm—and the night was dry and hot as the hob of Hell—this was the kind of port they were looking for. And they left their horses at the hitching rack, where there was a conveniently-placed, and full, water-trough, and they trooped on in.

The place was not full, as the night was yet young, and people were spaced around on the parked-dirt floor. There were rickety tables and equally rickety chairs and along the longest wall, the one right opposite the batwings was a long row of trestles on barrels, and this was the bar.

There was not a lot of conversation, but blue smoke hung under the low roof. The place had the appearance, and the *feeling*, Pete Ricken thought, of some kind of a hang-out, a place for conspirators, a *clan-place*.

You could feel the eyes on you—but you could not catch their owners looking.

And even the small buzz of conversation waned as the quartet entered.

Pete led the way to the bar.

People leaned on the bar and, whereas they had been looking at first, these people now studiously ignored the newcomers.

But Pete, who was nearest, thought he heard somebody murmur the word, 'Injun'.

Even then he could not possibly have foreseen what would happen, and how terribly far it would go.

But things started to speed up a bit then.

The whole effect up till then had been one of near-somnolence. The four men, slumped in the saddles of weary horses coming slowly into the settlement in the almost-night, in the heat that had a *thrumming* deepness. The men dismounting stiffly from the horses and stretching themselves with dreamlike moves and postures and the beasts drooping their heads to the brimming water-trough. The mens' heels scraping and clacking across the boardwalk without haste and the batwings swinging slowly and the lights meeting them so that they blinked their eyes as if suddenly awakened from sleep. . . .

The heat in here under the low roof was intense, enough to make anybody sleep. And when the other people moved they did not move much and there was indeed a dreamlike quality about it all.

63

But, so suddenly, the dream turned into a nightmare.

The barman was a cadaverous individual with red-rimmed eyes and an almost hairless pate. There was something ghoul-like about him. With quick eyes, Pete Ricken had noted those others about him. A mean and nasty and sorry bunch. A shifty-eyed, lip-licking conglomeration of human garbage.

God, I'm getting sour in my old age, Pete thought.

Maybe it's all down to that goddam Perrier!

Though, come to think of it, Perrier had not opened his mouth since they entered this place!

Perrier was almost at Pete's side actually, and Pete had his belly against the improvised bar when the cadaverous barkeep spoke.

He had a voice like a toad with tonsillitis and he said:

'I don't serve Injuns!'

The voice was pretty loud though, and all other voices ceased.

*　　　*　　　*

By nightfall Jasper and Hack had got themselves a nice double room—with two cots to boot—in the Mainsville Hotel.

They were not yet in the mood for sleeping, however. They went out to explore the town's nightlife, to sample some of its facets, the kind

64

of facets that were not available by day.

Jasper managed to drop quite a slice of their ill-gotten *dinero* in a game of chuck-a-luck, before Hack pulled him away.

And they were coming out of this particular gambling establishment when things started to happen.

A gunshot blasted out of the night and a slug plucked at Jasper's shirt near his right bicep.

Both men dived from the boardwalk, though in opposite directions.

Jasper had the cover of a water-butt which, luckily was half-full of dirty slops. He couldn't have done better for himself had he worn chain armour.

Hack was not so lucky. He sprawled flat on his belly in the meagre cover of a hitching-rack which only held one horse, a gaunt-ribbed sorry-looking nag who gave the pinwheeling man one sour look and then lost interest.

But, when Jasper, covering his friend, opened up with two guns this nag started to buck.

Then he started to scream. A blood-curdling sound. He had been hit. He kicked wilder and Hack had to scramble out of the way. He saw the beast's yellow teeth and rolling eyes in the light from a nearby window of the gambling hall. He could not bring his gun up. He could only lie out of the range of the flailing hooves and hope he didn't stop a bullet with his head.

The wounded horse collapsed suddenly, his

65

legs sprawling in all directions. He gave one last long bubbling sigh and then Hack knew he was dead. He spared a quick, sad thought for the poor beast. No Westerner likes to see a horse die. Then he was raising his gun.

But then there was more screaming; and it wasn't the horse this time, couldn't be!

Jasper's stream of fire had paid off—in spades!

This was a thinner animal sort of screaming which died in very much the same way, and then there was silence.

But, almost immediately somebody opened up again over there and bullets came perilously close to both Hack and Jasper. A window smashed; glass tinkled; a slug ricocheted from somewhere and sped away with a dying whine; a slug thunked into wood and Hack was showered with sharp chips.

Then he opened up.

There was no more screaming and, when the shooting died there was an almost-silence.

In the gambling-hall voices were raised excitedly. Down the street somebody shouted but there was not a soul in sight. When lead was flying only an idiot stuck his head out and Mainsville did not seem to have any actual idiots.

'Let's move, spread out,' said Hack softly.

'Right.'

But, even as they moved they both saw the

running man, both raised their guns and lowered them again.

The man had vanished.

The sound of bootheels faded in the night.

The two partners ran across the street. Hack went sprawling over something soft on the opposite board-walk; he had not been looking down, he had been looking ahead, hoping to catch another glimpse of the running figure. But then he saw the ghastly face in the light from a nearby window.

It was a face that in life had been very handsome but was twisted now in shock and agony, the lines imprinted on it by the *rigor* of death, the eyes staring, the mouth grimacing, the teeth bared in the way the poor horse's had been, lying there over on the other side of the street.

If this was the one who had shot the horse he had certainly paid for it. A bullet had ploughed into him at the base of his throat and blood spilled from there and trickled from his open mouth.

His right arm was in a white, now blood-spattered sling, but a gun lay near his left hand, so he had obviously been a two-shooter operator.

Jasper had turned back. 'Who is it?' he asked.

'The handsome boy. He's as dead as they come. He's suttinly the one who seems to stop all the lead.'

'And his friend is getting away.'

Jasper's words were echoed by mocking hoof-beats.

'Let's get after the bastard,' said Jasper.

They ran. They got their horses from the stables. But, by the time they got out on the plain and halted to listen, the sound of hoofbeats had died and there was only a faintly-soughing breeze which did little to temper the blood-thrumming of the furnace-heat.

'He's long gone,' said Hack. 'And I guess he ain't coming back. I vote we return to town, old-timer.'

'All right.'

On the edge of town a bulky figure awaited them on a standing horse. The levelled twin muzzles of a shotgun were plain to see.

'I want you two boys down at the jail,' said Marshal Jack Muldoon. 'You sort of have some explainin' to do.'

CHAPTER TEN

Missy Prentiss was part-owner of the Mainsville Hotel, the share bequeathed to her by her father at his death. Her father, as well as being the town mayor and good friend of Marshal Muldoon, had been by profession a hotelier, and a very good one.

His partner in the Mainsville establishment was an enormously fat man named Jacob Sanlee.

Jacob, a bachelor, had always been fat, but not enormously so—until about six years before his partner's death. The two men were of about the same age. It was a tragic coincidence that Jacob was rendered virtually helpless by an accident and then, six years later, his partner was killed in another accident, and not such a dissimilar one either.

Jacob was thrown from his carriage and trampled by his own two horses; his partner, Missy's father, was gored to death by a bull. Jacob now had the most palatial room in the hotel of which he was part-owner and sat in his bed against a frame which his doctor had had made for him by a local carpenter. Jacob could use his arms and he could move his head but the rest of him was immobilized and his legs were poor wasted things, his once-massive thews now sticks. The rest of him was enormously fat. It was Missy, now like the daughter he had never had, who unstrapped him from his frame at night and laid him down to rest. And, for the rest of the time he sat like a fat Chinese idol.

He was still a beaming, affable man, however, and constantly had friends to call. He was a wise and unfailingly cheerful old man. People brought their stories to him, and their problems also. An inveterate *raconteur* he never failed to cap their stories—and, more than likely he would solve their problems too.

Missy had a problem—of a sort.

She went to her Uncle Jacob with it.

An intelligent girl as well as a beautiful one, she told her story succinctly and, as was usual with him, the obese old man with the fat-encrusted wise and beady eyes listened gravely till she had finished.

Then he said:

'I think I know how you feel, honey. You feel guilty. Because the two boys ran foul of those fancy-pants gunslingers through sticking up for you, you now feel kind of responsible.'

'Yes, I suppose so. Isn't that natural though?'

'Yes, I suppose it is. According to what you've told me, however, I don't think Jack Muldoon has much to hold those two men for. Unless he's found out something about them that we don't know. You had never seen them before had you?'

'No-o.'

'They could be wanted for something, honey. But here in the West, as you well know, many of even the hardest nuts have a sense of chivalry about womenfolk,' Jacob grinned so widely his eyes completely disappeared, 'particularly pretty ones like you.'

The girl smiled in return, but there was still a doubtful look around her eyes and Jacob did not miss this, nor did he ignore it. And his features sobered again as he went on:

70

'I know and you know that Jack Muldoon is a very straight and conscientious man and, as a lawman, one of the best there is. And Jack goes by the book, as the saying is. You were a witness to the first shooting and you told your story to Jack and he accepted it. But there was no witness to the second shooting. To me it sounds like a drygulch set-up. But a man is dead and his partner has gone.

'If the partner had been caught he would be in jail with the other two strangers, you can bet any amount of dollars on that. Jack Muldoon doesn't play favourites. But he must hold an investigation. He doesn't know those two men, no more than you do. He has to hold them until he's sure that they were justified in the killing, just as much maybe as they were justified in the first shooting, the one you witnessed.

'But, in the absence of a witness to the second shooting, and a fatal one at that, Jack did what he had to do. You do see that don't you, honey?'

Missy's sense of humour got the better of her now and she laughed. 'My, Uncle Jacob,' she said. 'You do talk purty.' It was not the first time she had said this over the years, not by a long sight. In truth though, she loved to hear the old man talk in his deep, rumbling good-natured voice.

'Ask Jack Muldoon to come and see me,' the grinning Jacob said.

'He's gone out after the man who got away.'

'Oh, of course, he would do that, wouldn't he? But why didn't you tell me that before?'

'Didn't I? I'm sorry, Uncle Jacob.'

'No matter, honey. You go about your chores. I reckon Jack will be coming in here anyway when he gets back.'

'If that man's a killer, Marshal Muldoon will have to take care.'

Jacob rumbled, 'Jack used to eat two of that kind for breakfast every morning. You don't have to worry about him.'

'But if that man shoots from ambush like he did before?'

'You've got a point there. But old Jack will guard against such an eventuality, you can bet your boots on that.'

'All right, Uncle Jacob.'

Missy took her leave.

And, at about that time, Jasper, sharing a small cell with his friend, Hackwood, was saying, 'Kind of like old times ain't it, pardner?'

'Yeh, but we're in a bit of a box aren't we? If a posse happens along from that other town I mean.'

Jasper said: 'You've got a point there, oldtimer, I have to admit that.'

And from the front office the two prisoners could hear the tuneless whistling of the peglegged oldster called Jeremiah, who seemed to use a wicked-looking shotgun as a third leg and acted as deputy to Marshal Muldoon.

Although the prisoners did not know it for sure, there was a posse on their trail, the one led by troubleshooter Pete Ricken.

And they were in a sort of a box themselves right now.

★   ★   ★

Pete Ricken said: 'My friend ain't all Injun. You might call him a Dutchman.'

In the lowdown drinking dive in the lowdown town the cadaverous barkeep guffawed, not a merry sound.

'He don't look like a Dutchman to me,' the barkeep said.

After that there was a small silence, as if everybody was debating what to say, or what was to be said, next on the agenda. But, that this setting had something of the inevitability of a Greek Tragedy with the mischievous gods or fates in complete control, nobody could have foreseen. The habitués of this sinkhole were the scrapings of humanity. The four newcomers who had just arrived, including the 'Injun' that the barman had refused to serve, were white lilies by comparison.

But Pete Ricken, really, was no lily.

This was a fraught situation. But fraught situations were by way of being Pete's stock-in-trade. He wasn't called a troubleshooter for nothing. He met this situation in his usual way, head-on.

With his friends now grouped alongside him. His sidekick, young Bob Bendix, his tracker, Toledo, half-Indian, half-Dutch, his 'moaning Minnie' companion, Wells Fargo man Perrier.

And Pete took out his Colt and placed it on the dirty trestle bar before him, between him and the cadaverous barman and he said:

'Bucko, you will take our money and you will serve me and my three friends, including the Dutchman with the brown face whose name is Toledo and who is my tracker and my *compadre* from way back and has drunk with me in many bars.'

'Not in this one he ain't,' said the barman. 'And he ain't about to either.'

'There's no need for this, Mr Ricken,' put in the Wells Fargo man, Perrier. 'Let us go.'

Pete gave him an unemotional sidelong glance. 'You wanted a drink didn't you, Mr Perrier? You said you badly needed one, somep'n like that.'

'Yes, well, but....'

'All right....'

But in that split moment while Pete's attention had been diverted by the miserable-talking Perrier, the lank barman had acted with incredible swiftness, ducking, coming up again. And in his hand was a stubby sawn-off shotgun, the twin cut-down muzzles staring at the party at the other side of the trestled planks with

74

sightless yawning eyes.

'You'll turn about an' march out of here, all o' y',' the barman said.

'Don't point that thing at me,' said Pete Ricken and he picked up his gun and shot the cadaverous man in the shoulder.

The barman might not have been actually bluffing, but he certainly had not been set for shooting right off. In his bird-brain he had obviously opined that nobody but a maniac would go up against a loaded sawn-off at such close range: he had demonstrated that fact more than once in this little domain of his.

Now he was taken completely by surprise. It was as if a mule had kicked him in the shoulder with a hoof that was red-hot and smouldering. He was knocked backwards.

Involuntarily, his finger contracted on the trigger of the shotgun and it went off.

The Wells Fargo man, Perrier, screamed shrilly. He was knocked backwards far more violently than the barman had been and he fell flat on his back. His long legs twitched feebly a couple of times and then he became completely still.

Behind the bar the cadaverous man had passed out. The heavy revolver slug at close range had blown his shoulder to ribbons. Pete Ricken reached over quickly and picked up the shotgun and turned on the room.

Nobody else made a warlike movement.

75

Everybody seemed to be momentarily frozen. It had all happened too quickly!

Even Pete, now he had the situation in hand, seemed surprised at the violence he had unleashed.

Toledo bent over Perrier, rose immediately.

'He's dead, Pete.'

'Godamighty!'

Pete collected himself; he faced the assembled company and he spoke out.

'Any law here?'

A man nearby who sported a bushy pepper-and-salt beard and could have been any age between forty and seventy answered the question.

'Nope,' he said laconically.

Another man put in, 'A U.S. marshal calls once in a coon's age. That's all.'

There were assenting murmurs from other quarters. Now the noise had died and the suddenness, had been assimilated there was an air of settling-down. Nobody it seemed was going to loose a lot of energy or wind over a dead stranger, or even a wounded barman: any fool could pour liquor.

Things were still up to Pete Ricken, stranger or not. He seemed to be a jasper who had plenty of moxie and a whole lot of initiative to go with it. He was also a wizard with a six-gun, as he had amply demonstrated; and nobody was going to argue about *that!*

76

Pete said: 'Bob, you take Perrier's body back home, tell 'em what happened. I ain't turning back now. I'm going on after those robbers. Toledo, you go with Bob—they'll need another witness to corroborate his story.'

The half-bred looked at him without expression and said: 'I'm coming with you. If I don't you'll maybe lose the trail. One of them hombres is part-fox, you know that.'

There was no arguing with that!

Pete shrugged. 'All right, Toledo.' He turned to his sidekick. 'You be all right, Bob?'

'Guess I'll have to be,' said the young man phlegmatically.

Willing hands helped to lash the body to Perrier's own horse.

The people of the settlement were eager to see the back of this bunch.

Yeh, everything had happened very quickly, *terribly*.

How, even in his wildest nightmare, could the ever-complaining Wells Fargo man have contemplated his own death so suddenly and so terribly.

The cadaverous barman had regained consciousness and was being tended to by a few of his cronies.

The party that had brought about the Injun-hating individual's near-comeuppance wended their way from the settlement and then, without further debate split into two, Bob Bendix to return home with the burdened horse and Pete and Toledo to continue with their quest.

The night was hot and airless. . . .

CHAPTER ELEVEN

Marshal Jack Muldoon rode pretty hard. But he stopped from time to time to listen. The night was as black as the inside of a windowless dungeon, though changing from time to time as the hot stormclouds shifted and a few fugitive stars peeped shyly.

The heat seemed to blanket sound. So that a couple of times Jack dismounted from his horse and got down on his knees and then pressed his ear to the ground. Then he could hear, or so he thought, the faint drumming of hooves.

But, then again, it could well be only the *thrumming* of the heat.

He slowed down when he knew he was approaching the hills, long before he could actually see them in fact. But there were outcrops of rocks before that and a few sparse groves of trees. Any of these spots could make dry-gulch cover. Jack knew he had one advantage over his quarry though—the man could not possibly know as much about this territory as he did.

As much as possible Jack avoided rocks and

trees and finally, without mishap, he reached the foothills.

At first his horse, a nimble beast managed quite well but then, as the ground got steeper and more uneven Jack had to dismount and lead him. There were trails through here, of sorts, and Jack was using one of the best of them. They climbed, then dipped, then climbed again. This one had less ups and downs than most.

By daylight Jack might well have been able to follow the trail of the man he was following. He was a good tracker. Trampled scrub grass would have given him its story, newly-broken twigs, bruised herbs which raised a faint aroma. But, in this dark night Jack had no means of knowing whether the fugitive had taken this particular trail or not.

One thing was for sure, the man would have to go over the hills. He would not have had the time to double back or Jack would have got onto him for certain.

Jack knew that his approach could now be heard. Even covering the horse's hooves with soft strips of something would have been little help, for their journey, the scrabbling hooves, the scraping riding-boots, sent dirt and shale pitter-pattering down, sometimes even causing a clattering landslide. And the echoes here were long.

But the other fellow was in the same bind wasn't he? And, here again, Jack halted from time to time to listen.

He was upright and climbing, however, when he heard the horse whinny.

Jack's own horse pricked up his ears but did not reply to the shrill, neighing call.

Jack could imagine how that other beast's owner would curse. And Jack knew now the man was ahead of him, maybe on the same trail.

As he moved on upwards he tried to find cover, but that was more difficult now. His horse could not follow him onto the perilous places beside the trail.

By the sound when the other horse sang out Jack knew that his quarry could not be very far ahead of him and probably moving over dangerous terrain which he did not know.

Jack knew that ahead now there was a large outcrop of various boulders of various shapes and sizes, the product of a landslide ages ago and embedded there as if sprouting from the thin soil. If a man wanted to make a drygulch play this was the place to do it. So Jack ground-hitched his horse, knowing the beast would stay there until he heard a whistled signal to move.

Then the man veered off the trail and moved on slowly, in a half-crouch, his gun in his hand now.

Although no longer in his prime he was active and sure-footed. But he would have had to be a tripping fairy, not to dislodge shale and soil in his passing.

And, up ahead of him, from the boulders that crested the rise a gun opened up.

But, half-crouching, Jack had cover now also. He dropped to one knee behind a boulder of his own. But the bushwhacker's shooting was wide anyway: he had fired at sound rather than at shape, he had been too hasty.

Jack fired a couple of shots at the rock outcrop where it was limned against the sky. One of them ricocheted away with a high whine, awakening screaming echoes. The other spent itself somewhere. Jack did not imagine he had hit anything.

He dodged along to the other side of his cover. He had aimed to draw the other man's fire, and in this he succeeded.

Slugs spanged into the side of the boulder where Jack had been split moments before. The man up there was aiming better now. But he was aiming at the wrong place.

Jack moved out of cover at the end of the large boulder which had protected him up till now. He fanned the hammer of his gun, emptying it. He had a back-up gun, ready-loaded, in the other side of his belt. But he did not need it. As the echoes died, somebody was screaming.

Then the sound died, and there were not even any echoes, just the pattering and hissing of dust.

And up there a horse whinnied. It was a

81

plaintive sound.

Jack had gone back behind the cover of his boulder. The other man could be playing possum. Maybe that screaming had all been part of the act. It had seemed kind of overblown!

There was no real sound now . . .

Maybe night-noises, which seemed all part of the oppressive heat. Nothing identifiable or suspicious.

Up there the boulder outcrop, limned against a stormy sky only a shade lighter than the rocks looked like a monstrous prehistoric thing that might begin to crawl and slither at any moment. If a man looked at shapes like that for too long he could in fact imagine they were moving, as one, or splitting, spreading. . . .

Without sticking his neck out too far, Jack Muldoon fired one more shot. Then he waited till the echoes died and, in that short time nothing else happened.

Jack began to move. But, even then, like the old fox he was he did not move in a straight line. He made a short of detour and he still used all the cover he could find. He made noise; but he did not draw any more fire-power.

He did not, however, get back onto the sketchy trail until he was behind the large outcrop of boulders. And then he turned.

He saw the man slumped there.

That one was not playing possum!

Even in the night Jack Muldoon knew the

lineaments of death. He felt regret. Never had he been not able to feel regret, even when he gunned down an enemy. And this treacherous one would have shot him like a rattlesnake!

Reaching the body, he rolled it over. Then he was able to see that the man had stopped lead full in the chest, maybe more than one slug at that, the spreading blood black in the stormy night.

Jack whistled his horse who began to come up the steep trail. And from behind Jack there were other movements and the man turned and said softly 'Come on then, boy' and the dead bushwhacker's mount came tentatively forward out of the blackness.

The beast was soon reassured, particularly when Jack's own horse appeared.

Jack put the man's body over the saddle of the horse he had ridden and lashed it there with the coiled lariat he found over the saddle-horn. He used his jack-knife to cut another piece from the rope and he joined the two horses together with his own mount in the lead.

He led his cortège carefully down the rocky slopes.

He was halfway back to Mainsville when the skies opened and the long-threatened rain at last gushed down.

Jack kept on going.

It was a sodden man with an even more sodden corpse that woke up the local undertaker. But the little bald-headed corpse-keeper just loved new business! He said it was a pity the body was in such a mess.

But he loved his work too, and welcomed a challenge.

'You don't have to make him look like no saint,' said Marshal Muldoon. 'For that he ain't.' He took the horses down to the livery-stables where there was still somebody on duty and then he went from there to his own office.

Half an hour later, in dry clothes, with a couple of large belts of fair-to-middling rye whisky in his belly he was shepherding the two men from his jail-cell into the morgue to view the corpse.

The keeper of the cadaver was a little mortified: he hadn't had time to do much yet.

'Hell,' snorted the marshal. 'They only want to look at his face.'

They looked at his face and, contorted though it was it was still recognizable.

'That's the other one all right,' said Hack.

'Shore is,' said Jasper.

'What other one?' asked the undertaker.

The marshal said: 'He's the pardner of the one you have in the back room.'

'Oh, my,' said the little man. Then he added eagerly, 'He's ready. Do you want to look at him too?'

'We've seen him,' said Jasper laconically.

And that seemed to tie things up.

Outside, Jack Muldoon said: 'I'm accepting you boys' stories now. Hell, that one tried to drygulch me too, didn't he? I'm letting you go. But, if you stay in town I want you to endeavour to sing kind of small.'

'We get you, Marshal,' said Hack.

'We'll do as you ask,' said Jasper dutifully.

Hack said he wanted to go down to the stables to see his pinto.

Jasper said he hadn't seen his ol' mulehead for a while either.

They left the marshal standing there and, when they were out of earshot Jasper said:

'I'm in a sort of a mind-changing mood right now an' I'm not sure whether I want to stay in this town or not. I've had the tour, including the jail, and I ain't particularly impressed.'

'I can understand your mind-changing,' Hack said. 'But after seeing to the hosses I'm for supper and then some shut-eye. Let's sleep on things, pardner, huh?'

'Ain't no harm in that,' said Jasper.

CHAPTER TWELVE

The bald and cadaverous barman that walrus-moustached troubleshooter Pete Ricken had plugged in the shoulder in that dark dive of the miserable sinkhole in the prairie was known as

Latch.

He had two younger brothers called Vin and Ginger, who were on the owlhoot and used big brother Latch's drinking den as a base. They were out on some kind of skulduggery when Latch got himself shot. The fact that Latch had at the same time killed a man with his shotgun and maybe should be dead himself cut no ice with Vin and Ginger when they returned.

They were the last bitter remnants of a tight, feud-fighting clan—and Latch's shoulder was shot all to hell and, by the brothers' lights somebody had to pay for that.

The drunken old horse-doctor who served the settlement as its only medico had got the bullet out of the mangled shoulder, and quite a lot of shattered bone with it too. The man was a butcher, but he was better than nothing at all and you just had to take a chance on him. . . .

It was evident to everybody that Latch would never use his right arm again, might lose it altogether, might even lose his life.

Vin and Ginger, who knew a hell of a lot more about mayhem than they did about medicine decided they couldn't do much for their brother by just hanging around and cussing. It was up to them to put down the folk who did that to Latch. They had not got a big start and should be pretty easy to find, a quick-shooting oldster with walrus whiskers and a half-breed with a face like a brown nut.

They were bragging about this in the drinking den when somebody else spoke up from the back of the room.

'The oldster is called Pete Ricken. He used to have quite a rep as a lawman, an' all. I don't think he's toting a star now. Leastways, he didn't have one in plain sight yesterday. But he's still mighty bad medicine.'

All eyes sought out the speaker, a wizened oldster who was seldom sober.

'How do you know this jasper, Mullins?' asked Ginger.

'He sent me up once. He was just a sprig then but one o' the fastest guns I've ever seen. I had six months hard labour in Yuma.'

The other brother, Vin spun a coin towards the old man. 'Get yourself a drink, Mullins,' he said magnanimously. 'Come on, Ginger, let's ride.'

They did not bother to check on Brother Latch again before they left. Killing was their business, not kind words.

'Fastest gun he's ever seen,' snorted Vin, his dark head next to his brother's slightly older ginger one. 'When I catch up with that gunslinger an' his Injun friend I'll stitch 'em up every-which-way before they can even blink.'

Ginger guffawed. 'An' I'll blow their heads off,' he said.

Brother Latch had done a lot of guffawing before he was put down. Guffawing sort of ran in the family, which never had the right amount of brains to go round, just more than its rightful share of pure, murderous *meanness*.

'I'll tell you somep'n else, Vin,' Ginger went on.

'Do tell, brother.'

'While you wuz out in the privy earlier one of the boys told me somep'n else.'

'What then, f'r Chrysakes?'

'Seems like that sharp-shooting Ricken bastard asked about two men who might have rode by earlier. Seemed like this bunch wuz chasin 'em. Two men, one of 'em riding a pinto.'

'Anybody see those two, an' the pinto?'

'They didn't say.'

'It's somep'n to remember though, huh?'

'That's what I thought.'

★ ★ ★

'The next town on this trail is a place called Mainsville,' said Pete Ricken. 'But it's quite a piece yet.'

'Those two seem to be headin' that way,' said Toledo. 'But we can't keep riding forever. We went right through the night and we ain't seen a thing, heard a thing.'

'You think we ought to light down for a spell then, make a bit of fire, brew some coffee.'

'Ain't so much chance of a fire being spotted

now,' said Toledo. 'Not with the light and the morning sun. Anyway, we can see for miles. How 'bout trying that bunch o' trees over there?' The half-breed pointed.

'Yeh, that's cover all right. Not so much chance of a fire being spotted. And a good look-out point. You still think some o' that barman's friends might want to follow us an' even things?'

'It's possible, though they were a pretty sorry bunch. Anyway, it don't do to take fool chances.'

'You never did, did you, yuh ol' Piute?' said Pete.

'I ain't no Piute.' Toledo grinned, revealing a row of broken, tobacco-stained teeth. 'I spit on Piutes. Any Apache could lick six of 'em. Me an' my Dutch ancestors spit on all Piutes.'

'Got you goin' again didn't I?'

'Like you aimed to, you English heathen.'

'My ancestors were Scots.'

'Wild heathens!'

'There's a lot of us in the West.'

'Wild heathens,' repeated Toledo. 'You ought to join up with my Apache ancestors.'

'That's a thought,' said Pete. 'Between 'em we could lick the whole goddam United States, including the Dutchmen.'

They were both laughing as they rode into the grove of trees. They dismounted. Toledo began to gather sticks for the fire. Pete broke out their meagre provisions. Pete said:

89

'Come to think of it, if we rest here for a piece and then go on we should hit Mainsville in the heat of the afternoon when most folk are kind of drowsy. And if those two bozos we're looking for are there we'd have a better chance to catch 'em on the hop.'

'I figure they had some storm out there last night,' said Toledo. 'Remember the thunder we heard last night an' the sheet lightnin' we saw? Thataway! It's still dark in the skies up that way too, and I figure it's coming our way now.'

They both gazed out at the stormclouds massing in the opposite direction from where they had come. The heat was intense and the sun above them was brassy.

By the time they had finished their coffee and a few warm handfuls of beans on tin plates there was no sun and there was an artificial night which had a vapour-like blueness about it like the massed fumes of tons of smouldering dynamite.

The rain came as a welcome relief, gushing down like a waterfall. The trees were not much shelter against it, but the two men did not care about this. In seconds they were soaked to the skin and they both took their shirts and pants off. Already in bare feet, they capered a bit under the rain and their horses, although they seemed to welcome the rain too, eyed their masters in wonderment.

Grotesque in baggy, much-washed long johns

they linked arms and did a minuet and then broke apart and danced their own private kinds of fandangos, like men did at festive times in many of the camps and settlements where there were no women.

'Best goddam bath you've had since you were a papoose,' yelled Pete.

'Are you insinuating that I'm a dirty Injun?' demanded Toledo.

Pete laughed uproariously over the loud drumming of the rain and did a clumsy cartwheel, finally landing on his butt in the grass.

'A dirty Dutchman,' he yelled.

'Horse-manure!' yelled Toledo and sat down opposite him.

They sat looking at each other and grinning like kids while the puddles gathered around them.

When the rains came, the two brothers, Vin and Ginger were caught right in the middle of the plains with no shelter in sight. They struggled into their slickers and ploughed on, cursing their restive horses.

They shouted across at each other.

Vin suggested that they turned back.

Ginger, who was the most cantankerous of the two, said they would get just as wet either way.

When they had returned to the settlement after pulling their last job, a trading post stick-up, they had hoped to rest awhile, drink some of the better liquor that Brother Latch kept for them, stuff themselves with food, sample the favours of various of the women who hung around the settlement like vultures awaiting juicy pickings.

But Latch had had to get himself shot.

And they, his dutiful brothers, had had to go out after the folk who had done it and seek vengeance.

'I guess mebbe Latch asked for it,' Vin shouted at his brother now above the driving rain. 'He's too damn' fond of pointing that pesky shotgun of his'n at other folk.'

'Well, they didn't have to shoot him,' shouted Ginger.

'He shot one o' them.'

'But that was after—sort of an accident. That was what I was told anyway.'

'Yeh, I guess,' said Vin. 'Me too. I heard. . . .'

'I can't hear you,' yelled Ginger. 'What in hell are you muttering about?'

'Makes no never-mind,' yelled Vin, nastily, and he nudged his horse a little further away from the other man.

He hated this goddam rain! Latch had got them into this, him and his itchy trigger-finger!

They plodded on, not shouting at each other now, not even exchanging disgusted glances. If they uttered obscenities under their breath the fury of the storm made the words puny things.

92

CHAPTER THIRTEEN

Jasper said: 'After breakfast, that's when we ought to get moving. It don't sit right with me now, us staying here. We're loose now and we want to stay loose. Jack Muldoon is a smart man. He's bound to think some more about the way we handled ourselves with those two fancypants, although neither of 'em are alive now to tell the tale and Jack himself was responsible for half o' that.

'Your face ain't known, but mine is. I ain't seen anybody in this town yet that looks familiar to me—but somebody might have spotted me who knows me from way back. And it only needs one word to Muldoon.'

'I'm not riding in all this rain,' said Hack.

'After breakfast I said. It might ease off by then. I do swear the sky is getting lighter.'

'Hell's bells, I've seen better skies in the middle of a dust-storm.'

They were still arguing in a bantering sort of way as they went down the stairs.

Most of all they were hungry.

Missy served them herself, said jokingly that she was glad they were still managing to keep out of jail.

'Durn tootin',' said Jasper.

Hack was a bit preoccupied. He knew his

partner was right: they should get moving. But he knew also that something had *passed* between the beautiful, red-headed girl and himself, something completely innocent as yet, but there all the same.

This girl, however, was no bored and amorous rancher's daughter. He figured that she did not have the time or the inclination for cheap dalliance. He liked women very much and had always found it easy to make most of them like him. But he hadn't got himself hogtied again yet. Missy was the first woman who had interested him seriously since he lost his wife.

He felt he wanted to stay around this red-headed girl, stay in this town, see what happened. His feelings about a woman lately had never been this mixed up, but a whole lot more basic. It surprised him to realize that, with this girl, he didn't want them that way. And he had known her such a short time too; they were not even on first-name basis yet.

But that could soon be remedied, he thought.

Her gaze on him was warm and he looked up at her from the table and he tried it: 'How are you this morning, sweet Missy.'

You mealy-mouthed bastard, Hackwood, he thought.

But she smiled and looked at him levelly as if to say 'I like you, mister, but don't give me any soft-soap'. What she did say, however, was:

'I'm fine this morning, Mr Hackwood. How

94

are you?'

'I'm fine too, thank you. And my friends call me "Hack".'

Not to be outdone, the other man at the table said: 'And my friends call me "Jasper".'

She chuckled. It was a feminine sound, yet throaty. 'I knew that already of course,' she said. 'Jasper and Hack. What a combination!'

Then her face sobered again and Hack thought that, in repose, it was the most beautiful face he had ever seen. Maybe she was thinking that the combination could be a lethal one, as the handsome young stranger had discovered. And his body lay beside his friend's down at the morgue right now.

The fat waitress signalled her and, with another quick and rather impersonal smile in the direction of the two men, she went back across the dining-room.

She walks the way she looks, thought Hack, and that's beautiful too.

Jasper said: 'I know what you're thinking. And I know, and you know, that we have got to go.'

'You don't know all I'm thinking, pardner.'

That seemed to end the conversation. They ate. And a little later, his mouth not quite empty of prime ham, Jasper said:

'I'll sure miss the chow here.'

'Me too,' said Hack and that seemed to clinch things. They both knew they would be moving

95

soon.

And, at last the rain was abating.

They did not see Missy again before going back to their room; leastways, not to talk to. The dining-hall had been very busy and when she was not hidden in the kitchen she moved quickly and they caught glimpses of her from time to time.

They got their gear ready and took it down to the stables.

Without words, they seemed to have come to yet another tacit agreement, and that was not to say *adios* to anybody, just to leave, and hope that nobody important saw them go and wanted to ask questions.

But they didn't see anybody they remembered seeing before—only the old hostler, and he saw people coming and going all the time and never asked questions.

He *was* asked questions though—people always seemed to want to know what lay over the next hill.

And if he had told them that one valley looked pretty much the same as another one and, when they got to his age all valleys blended into one and there were no more hills, they would've looked at him like he was crazy in the head.

He watched those two gunslingers go. They had only been in Mainsville for a hoot and a holler, but already they had killed a man and spent a night in jail. He wondered if either of them would live as long as he had. He doubted it!

Anyway, it had stopped raining at last. So they wouldn't get wet. The sun was shining brightly.

They were outside of town when Jasper said: 'I wonder if we will ever see that place again.'

And, for the first time, Hack realized the loneliness of the owlhoot life.

★   ★   ★

The sun was shining and the world looked sparkling and new after the rain.

Pete Ricken and his half-breed friend, Toledo, were far from being overdressed and their clothes soon dried.

They saw the town ahead of them, like black toy bricks thrown down on a sparkling green baize expanse.

Perhaps the bricks were dice and this was a new game!

But the game that Pete and Toledo were soon about to undertake was far grimmer than anything that could be evolved from pitching dice, even funeral-looking black ones.

'I guess that's Mainsville,' said Pete.

'Yeh.'

They went on a little further. They were not pushing themselves now. Then Toledo said:

'Hold hard, Pete.'

And he was shading his eyes with his hand and looking ahead.

Their horses, abreast, came to a halt.

'You see somep'n, Toledo?'

'Two riders. Comin' from the town. Comin' right towards us.'

'Yeh, I see them now, pard. Hell, you've got eyes like a turkey buzzard. They're mighty indistinct to me, and they don't seem to be in any kind of a hurry.'

'I can't see them all that plain, Pete. They seem to be slowing down, as if they're tryin' to make up their minds about somep'n.'

'Mebbe they've spotted us.'

'I don't think so.'

Although Toledo did not know it, he had been right in his half-assumption that the two riders in the distance were trying to make up their minds about something. They were in fact having a slight argument.

'I tell you,' Hack said, 'we're going the wrong way. We're almost going back the way we came.'

'I don't think so, pard,' said Jasper. 'I know of a settlement where we can lay low, and it's in this direction.

'Well, we must have passed near to it before then, maybe just out of sight.'

'I don't think so. Anyway, if we are doubling-back a bit, it is only a little way and if anybody is tailing us they could be thrown off the

98

scent. . . .'

'Or we could run straight into 'em.'

'Hell, I don't suppose they actually know us anyway,' said Jasper.

'You sure don't mind taking chances, do you?'

'You've got to take chances sometimes in this game. Anyway, once we get to this settlement I'm talkin' about we can sit pretty for a while. There's a shebang there run by a character called Latch. His two brothers, Vin and Ginger are on the owlhoot and I know them of old, though I ain't actually recommending them. They're a poisonous pair. But big brother Latch will hide out anybody, with plenty of eats, booze, women, and nobody 'ull get any information from that town.'

'Why didn't we go there before Mainsville then?'

'We didn't know we were gonna shoot anybody in Mainsville did we? We didn't know Marshal Jack Muldoon was gonna get leery. Like I said before, we're loose now and we suttinly want to stay loose. But I've got a sneaking suspicion we're not right out o' the woods yet.'

'Mebbe you're right,' said Hack. 'Hell, you're the expert. I'll go along.'

'I ain't no expert,' said Jasper. 'Just a dirty ol' fox who has been hunted before.'

As they rode on Hack said: 'You know, while

you were talking I thought I saw a couple of riders up ahead. Long ways away, but they looked like riders all right. Not just cattle or grazing horses.'

'Cowhands maybe.'

'Maybe. I can't see them now.'

Jasper shaded his eyes. 'I can't see anything neither. Not even cattle or horses. There are a few trees up ahead though, so if they were cowhands they could have gone into shelter and hunkered down for a smoke.'

'Yeh. Best keep our eyes peeled even so—an' our wits about us.'

'Hell, you're as jumpy as an old maid with her drawers full of bees.'

Hack said darkly, 'Howmsoever...' And he didn't finish his sentence.

CHAPTER FOURTEEN

Pete and Toledo were not cowhands, but they were indeed hunkered down among the trees and looking out.

And finally, watching the approaching riders, Pete said:

'Judas Priest! One of 'em is riding a pinto.'

'Can we be sure they're the two people we're looking for?' said Toledo. 'They seem to be sort of doubling-back.'

'Maybe that's deliberate,' said Pete Ricken.

'They certainly seem to fit the descriptions we have,' said Toledo. 'Sketchy though they were. An' that pinto is a real little beauty.'

'Mount up,' said Pete. 'We will ride out and challenge those two. No shooting though, unless you have to. We wouldn't want to make any mistakes. Pinto or no pinto!'

'I'm with you, Pete.'

They rode out of the trees, spacing themselves apart, but not too noticeably so. They did not want this to look like the set-up it actually was.

The two approaching riders looked wary and capable, but they looked relaxed also.

The elder of the two looked somehow familiar to Pete Ricken.

He looked like a hardcase and Pete had had plenty of experience with hardcases.

His companion was probably not much younger, and lean and hardbitten. But, somehow, there was more of the look of a working cowhand about him.

But the other! Yeh, Pete knew *his* stamp.

Pete was nothing but forthright, alarmingly so.

He reined in his horse across the dimly-defined trail and he said:

'You two boys know anything about a payroll grab that happened back-aways?'

It was not till afterwards that he realized how

stupid he had been—and he also remembered who the older of the two men was . . . .

For it was this man who moved, and Pete, a fast man himself, was taken by surprise. A burn-assed rattlesnake could not have struck any faster.

While Pete was speaking, Toledo had reached surreptitiously for the rifle in his saddle-boot, and the drawing man's shot was aimed at him.

Toledo's horse screamed in agony as a slug burned its neck. It reared high and, fine rider though he was Toledo was thrown from its back.

As Pete Ricken reached for his gun, Toledo's horse cannoned into Pete's own mount and, gun in one hand Pete had to do some fancy work with the reins in his other in order to stay in the saddle and quieten the startled beast at the same time. He could not aim his gun, let alone shoot it.

He heard one of the two other men shout 'Come on!' He did not know which one it was. Then they streaked past, lying low over their saddles and screeching like Indians.

Pete managed to quieten his own beast and he took up his rifle and tried to get a bead on one or the other of the fleeting horsemen. But shooting from the saddle with a long gun is not comfortable, even from a standing horse, and Pete's two shots only burned the breeze.

The two horsemen were going like hounds

102

out of hell. A try with a handgun would have been wasted. Pete quickly slid from the saddle and got down on one knee in the grass.

God, I wish I had my old Sharps, he thought, I'd only have time for one shot but it might be the one to count, for that was a powerful, *reaching* long gun. As it was, with his Winchester repeating rifle he managed to squeeze off two shots, neither of which made the slightest difference to the progress of the fleeing men, so maybe they were out of range after all.

'Goddamit,' said Pete and turned his attention to his partner.

Toledo was on his feet and he was unhurt. His horse was standing trembling, blood running down its neck.

'It's just a crease luckily,' the half-breed said. 'I'll fix it. I think he's scared more'n anythin' else and that'll pass.'

Toledo bent and began to scan the ground. He tore up a clump of moss and pressed it gently to the horse's neck and, gradually the bleeding slowed and finally seemed to stop.

But Toledo remained beside the horse with the improvised poultice pressed to the wound and continued to talk softly to the beast.

Its trembling ceased. It looked enquiringly at its master.

'All right, *amigo*,' said Toledo, and he was obviously talking to the horse. 'We go on, huh?'

The beast made a little sound in his throat.

103

'He says it is all right,' remarked Toledo and he gave one of his rare grins, lighting up his dark face.

'So we go after those bozos, huh?' said Pete Ricken.

By way of answer Toledo mounted up and turned his horse about.

Then, side by side once more the two riders set off the way they had come.

Their quarry was out of sight.

'I think mebbe they're making for that settlement,' said Toledo.

'That certainly could cause complications,' said Pete laconically.

★   ★   ★

'I know that walrus-moustached oldster from way, back,' said Jasper. 'He's a lawman called Pete Ricken.'

'He didn't seem to be wearing a badge.'

'Maybe he wouldn't bother, not on the trail. As I remember Pete was never no book-lawman.'

'Whatever,' said Hack, 'he seemed to be after us, him an' his half-breed pard.'

'That one,' said Jasper. 'A tracker if I don't miss my guess. And a good one. I thought I had covered our trail pretty well.'

'Maybe they got lucky.'

'An' more than that.' Jasper seemed to be

aggrieved.

He went on: 'Maybe Pete Ricken don't need a badge. Maybe he ain't a honest-to-goodness official badge-toter anymore. Maybe he's a bounty hunter or a troubleshooter an' he's been sicced on to us. Badge or not though, he's still a mighty dangerous customer to have on our trail.'

'Well, we got past him, didn't we? Him and his tracker pard! And they weren't no posse. And where is this settlement-type hidey-hole you were telling me about?'

'It ain't far ahead.'

'There's somebody else coming,' said Hack. 'Up ahead.'

'Godammit, this is gettin' t' be monotonous.'

'We're wide open here. But then again, so are they. There isn't any good cover for miles.'

'So maybe they're just harmless pilgrims. So we'll act that way too.'

'That's what I feel like now, a pilgrim.'

They slowed down. They did not want to give the impression they were being chased.

The other two riders seemed to be slowing their progress too.

'Watch yourself, old hoss,' said Jasper. 'Maybe these are posse-members sort off, pards of Pete Ricken's who've been back-checking, maybe at the settlement, Latch's place. Then again, maybe they're hardhats just come out of Latch's place and have as much reason to be wary of strangers as we have.'

To be wary at all times, that was the owlhooter's creed, thought Hack. He was learning fast and he was learning hard. He could have got himself perforated back there. And now here was more uncertainty, coming from the front again. A man could get swivel-eyes and a twitchy trigger-finger.

He was only glad it was daylight and bright after the recent rains, and not in the deeps of night when a man could be shot down suddenly and left to die in the dark.

'I know them,' said Jasper. 'Ugly reprobates that they are. Them's Latch's two younger brothers, Vin and Ginger.' He raised his hand and gave a half-wave half-salute.

The other two brought their horses to a halt. There was a gap between them. They were wary pilgrims all right. And not just pilgrims, Hack figured. Not if they were past acquaintances of Jasper!

They peered past their horses' necks.

Then they both raised a hand in salutation.

The two mounted pairs came together.

Introductions were made and Hack found himself shaking hands with two of the most villainous-looking cutthroats he had ever seen, and that was saying something in this wild land!

'How's Latch?' Jasper wanted to know.

'He got himself shot,' said the brother with the ginger hair.

'Do tell!'

'Yeh, that's why we're makin' this way,' said the other brother. 'We're after the folks responsible. A walrus-moustached oldster who's supposed to be called Ricketts or somep'n like that....'

'Ricken,' put in Jasper.

The talking brother's eyes bugged a little. They looked mean. 'Ricken. Why...?'

'Latch ain't dead is he?'

'Nope. But he's got a mighty bad shoulder.'

'Maybe he'll get his revenge for that sooner than he thinks,' said Jasper.

CHAPTER FIFTEEN

'They didn't say goodbye,' said Missy. 'Not a proper goodbye.'

'What do you mean, *they?*' said the fat man. 'Time back you wouldn't have given the time of day to the older one. Why should you worry about him not saying *adios?*'

The girl laughed. 'Now you're teasing me, Uncle Jacob. I'd give the time of day to anybody, you know that. You're exaggerating.'

Jacob Sanlee shrugged enormous shoulders, all his fat vibrating and his merry eyes disappearing in rolls of pink flesh.

He said: 'Time of day.' He spread pink paws.

'Anybody can say "Hallo" to anybody. But I figure you would like to say a leetle more than "Hallo" to the younger one of those two ginks. I think you kind of took a shine to him.'

Missy tossed her auburn curls. 'Oh, you!' She could not be mad with Jacob Sanlee; she loved him too much.

And, in her heart of hearts, she knew the fat man was right in what he had said. She had taken a shine to the man called Hack. And she had sensed that he had taken a shine to her also. She did not think her womanly intuition had been at fault.

Consequently, it was all the more puzzling that he should have left Mainsville without even saying to her a formal goodbye.

Maybe he planned to return.

She went downstairs. Marshal Jack Muldoon was crossing the lobby and turned to greet her. They went together into the dining-hall where Muldoon seated himself at his favourite table.

It was not until half-an-hour or so later that the marshal said to Missy, 'Looks like our two friends have left, huh?' And she knew who he meant.

'Yes,' she said.

And Jack had not smiled; nor did he when he spoke again; there was a thoughtful look on his weather-beaten visage as he said:

'And not even a short *adios!*'

He's suspicious, thought Missy; why *would*

108

he be suspicious? Maybe it was just because he was a good lawman and, for better or worse, Jasper and Hack were two fiddlefoots. Jack would probably think of them as 'saddle-tramps'. She did not tell him that the two boys had not said goodbye to her either.

Write 'em off, you red-headed ass, she told herself. Forget 'em. Their sort never settled! What on earth had she been thinking of, for Pete's sake?

★   ★   ★

'Four of 'em,' said Toledo. 'I'm sure I saw four of 'em.'

'Well, if you say so, lynx-eyes,' said Pete Ricken. 'You ain't had a drink for days so you can't be seeing double. Two of 'em are the two we're after, we do know that. But who are the other two? Lemme think.'

'They're making for the settlement all right,' said Toledo, and then he shut up.

Then Pete said: 'The other two must be two of Latch's friends and they were after us. And they're acquainted with the two skunks we're chasing an' they've joined forces....'

'Figurin' all they've got to do now is go back to the settlement and wait?'

'Yeh, like fat spiders waiting for the flies.'

'You an' me being the flies?'

'Somep'n like that.'

Pete went on: 'Come to think of it, those two others boys could be Latch's brothers, Vin and Ginger. I ain't sure there'd be anybody else in that sinkhole willing to stick their necks out towards you an' me just on behalf of Latch who doesn't give nothing to nobody. But the two brothers are a different mess o' fish. They're a mighty tight clan, what's left of 'em.'

'So that's four at least,' said Toledo. 'Do you think anybody else would take a hand, if we rode in that is?'

'I guess not. Folks are at the settlement to lay low, not to poke their heads out. But we're outnumbered by two to one anyway, pardner, and those ain't sodbusters up there. Vin and Ginger are killers. And those other two can handle themselves. I recognised the one called Jasper. A hardcase from way back.

'No, Toledo, you an' me would be plumb foolish to go riding in there like they expect us to, making a big grandstand play. Like as not we'd probably both get our heads blown off.'

'Yeh,' said Toledo.

He added reflectively, 'Mebbe the two we were after 'ull ride right through.'

'I doubt it. Why would they? They've got a chance now to eliminate us for good and all. And then they can hole up in the settlement, quiet, until they want to move on.'

'Yeh, I see that, Pete. You're talking horse-sense all right. So what do we do?'

110

'First off we'll wait for dark.'

'I heard tell us Injuns ain't supposed to fight in the dark.'

'Horse-shit! You'll fight, and you'll put up with it, dark or no dark.'

Toledo chuckled. He said, parrotlike, 'I'll fight, and I'll put up with it, dark or no dark. Hell, I might even like it.'

*   *   *

Latch was propped-up in bed.

His face looked like a death's head.

He was mis-shapen with the bandages on his wounded shoulder, bandages already crimson in patches as the blood seeped through. The old horse-doctor had not seemed to be able to stop the blood, although Latch's brothers had threatened to slit the old man's throat if he didn't do something soon.

It seemed impossible that the cadaverous Latch should have so much red blood in him.

The doctor said privately to Hack that he thought Latch would probably die. Then he blinked red-rimmed rye-sodden eyes at the newcomer and pleaded with him not to tell the sick man's brothers.

'Those two maniacs mean what they said. They'll murder me.'

'I won't tell them,' promised Hack, wondering why the old soak had confided

111

in him.

Maybe the oldster saw that Hack was not of the same stripe as Vin and Ginger—thank the stars for that, Hack thought. Vin and Ginger were poisonous reptiles and no mistake, and their wounded brother wasn't much better. Hack wondered what the old man—he was well-pickled now but could once have been wise— thought about Jasper.

As for Vin and Ginger, they seemed to accept Jasper, just as they had done on the trail after the initial surprise-impact had faded. He was one of their kind. Well, almost!

But they were still a mite wary around Jasper's new pard, Hackwood, who, as far as they knew had no rep.

Then Jasper told them that him and Hack had been in jail together and that seemed to make them a bit less vinegary.

Latch said: 'Those two are pros. If they come they'll come by night.' Sick man or not, the cadaverous saloon keeper was still thinking straight. He could be as ruthless and cruel as either of his brothers, but he was no idiot.

'So we'll wait,' said Ginger.

And Vin laughed, a crazy, neighing sort of sound.

'We're with you,' said Jasper.

Hack did not say anything.

The doctor said: 'Latch ought to sleep now.' In order to save his own skin, the old man was still pretending he knew what he was about.

The four men left the room.

The light was beginning to fail.

Jasper said: 'If those two are cagey they'll maybe make a detour and come in the other end of town from the way we did.'

'Maybe they won't come at all,' said Hack. 'Seeing as how they're outnumbered.'

Vin said petulantly, 'Hell, I hope they come.'

Ginger said: 'If they don't, I guess we'll have to go out after them again.'

Next to Latch, Ginger was the elder brother by a year or two. He was cantankerous and treacherous, but he seemed a little more sensible than Vin. Anyway, Vin took notice of him.

Ginger seemed to be assuming command.

Jasper and Hack, playing their cards close to their vests, let the red-headed man get on with it. They were in his bailiwick.

He said: 'We'll split up. Me an' Vin at that end of town,' he pointed, 'you two at the other end.'

'Suits us,' said Jasper quickly.

Hack did not say anything.

Ginger said: 'If one of us spots 'em, we give a hoot-owl.'

Vin sniggered. 'An owl-hoot!'

'All right, an owl-hoot. Can you do an owl-hoot, Jasper?'

'None better.'

'Can you do an owl-hoot, Mistuh Hackwood?'

113

'I reckon.'

The two pairs separated.

Darkness fell rapidly and with it came a soughing breeze.

For about an hour Jasper and Hack heard nothing, but the breeze and a few fugitive noises from the town behind them. It was a secretive town, not a noisy one. It was not really a town, maybe more of a hidey-hole.

Then they heard the owl-hoot, clear as a bell tolling in the distance. More than once.

The visitors did seem to have made a detour.

'Unless it's just a pair of innocent pilgrims,' said Hack.

'I wouldn't want those two hellions to shoot no innocent pilgrims,' said Jasper. 'We better go find out.'

They joined the two brothers.

All were well-hidden.

And they heard the horses, not being ridden hard, but coming steadily nearer, steadily towards a hail of lead.

And, rising suddenly, Hack said: 'I'm not joining in a drygulch set-up like this.'

Then Vin had his gun on him and hissed, 'I'll blow your goddam head off.'

Hack's gun was still holstered. It was too late for him to draw.

'Don't fire a shot, you jackass,' hissed Ginger. 'Stick him.'

Vin rose, drawing his knife with his other

114

hand.

'No,' said Jasper. 'Take his weapons an' tie him an' gag him an' lock him up someplace.'

'Yeh,' said Ginger. 'If you stick him he might yell anyway.' He rose. 'Hell, c'mon will you, they're getting nearer.'

'I didn't figure it like this, Hack,' said Jasper.

Hack did not say anything.

CHAPTER SIXTEEN

Toledo was riding one horse and leading the other.

Pete had dismounted a little way back and was skirting the town on foot.

They had figured that there might be men waiting at each end.

Toledo was to give Pete as much time as possible, short of showing himself, getting himself shot.

Then Toledo was to let one horse go, though not right at the main drag.

They did not want to get a good horse all shot up, not if they could help it. They just wanted to create a diversion, so that they could both move into the settlement in one direction or another. Maybe then they could shoot their enemies, while taking care that, in the darkness they did not shoot each other.

It was a daring plan and certainly not a foolproof one. But they were both men used to taking chances, sometimes reckless ones. And these were reckless ones.

Maybe, though, this was the kind of recklessness the other side would not be expecting.

'Through and out,' Pete had said. 'Kill one or two. We certainly can't capture 'em now. Then out, drawing the others after us.'

'Watch for the riderless horse, for Pete's sake,' Toledo had said. 'It'll be yourn.'

'I'll get him. He's well-trained.'

They were ready for their desperate ploy.

★   ★   ★

'That's it,' said Marshal Jack Muldoon.

He was talking to himself.

Or, it could be said, he was talking to a 'dodger', as 'Wanted' notices were called the length and breadth of the lawless West.

The West being what it was, there were plenty of dodgers floating around, and Muldoon had had to go through a drawer full of them in his old oak desk before he found one that interested him.

'That's him all right,' said Muldoon.

And this time he wasn't talking to himself. Not exactly. He was overheard. His ancient peg-legged deputy, Jeremiah, entering the office

116

then; said:

'What in tarnation are you mumbling about.'

The marshal held the Wanted notice in front of the old man, stabbed a finger at it.

'Look at that. See if it reminds you of somebody.'

'Don't shove it on my nose then. Wait till I get my specs out.'

'They're on top of your head as usual,' the marshal snorted. 'I wonder you don't get more breakages. You...'

His voice tailed off. Jeremiah wasn't listening. He was peering at the dodger. He was not nearly as senile as he sometimes pretended to be.

He said now, sharply, 'The stranger. One o' those two. The one who's going bald. They burned down that fancypants. I figured they might be owlhooters. The drawing don't look much like him. . . .'

'They never do,' put in Muldoon.

Jeremiah gave him a peevish look. 'The description certainly fits though, an' they've got plenty information on him, including that he spent some time in Yuma Jail. He's got quite a sheet too. Murder. Robbery. . . .'

'And the name clinches it, doesn't it. Jasper Spinks. I didn't know his name was Spinks.'

'He did call himself Jasper though, didn't he?'

'Yup.'

117

'They lit a shuck out o' here though, didn't they, Jack?'

'Yup.' The marshal was being his old laconic self again. He was obviously thinking.

'Did you find anything about the other feller, Jack?' Jeremiah persisted. 'The one who called himself Hack?'

'Nope. But, riding with a long-standing hardhat like Jasper, he can't be no pantywaist.'

And Missy seemed to take a regular shine to that one, the marshal thought. Why, even Missy's 'Uncle Jacob' commented on that only yesterday.

Had that been his (Muldoon's) other reason for suddenly searching painstakingly through a whole pile of dusty, forgotten dodgers?

If so, he thought now, Hell, why not?

An owlhooter like Hack, friend of Jasper, would be no good to any girl, and Missy was a peach among girls: Jacob wasn't the only 'uncle' she had: since her dad died all her dad's old friends had to look out for the beautiful, red-headed, kind-hearted girl!

'It shouldn't be hard to find out which way they went after they left Mainsville,' Muldoon said. 'Somebody must have seen them go.'

'You going after them?'

'It's my job, ain't it?'

★   ★   ★

118

The approaching horses suddenly broke into a gallop.

And there was an Indian-yelling!

The horses seemed to have separated. The sounds in the night were very confusing. And that wild screeching was something of the kind that none of the waiting men had heard since they were boys. It made a body's blood run cold.

'They're trying to flank us,' Jasper yelled.

He fired over to the right. Vin and Ginger seemed to be firing in other directions. Jasper thought he saw a horse. Then it disappeared.

It had seemed to be riderless. Had one of the attackers already been hit? If so it must have been a lucky shot from one of the three of them.

Jasper missed Hack. But Hack could not, *would not* take a hand in this shindig.

There was firing from over to the left of Jasper. The Indian screeching had seemed to be coming from that direction. But you had to allow for echoes. And the screeching had stopped now anyway, and there was only the echoing blatter of gunfire.

Jasper heard Vin grunt explosively behind him.

Jasper turned.

Vin was slowly tipping sideways and Jasper scrambled out of his way. Vin fell on his side and rolled sluggishly, came to rest with his face turned towards Jasper.

Vin's eyes were staring but sightless and there was a hole in the side of his head from which thick blood, black in the night, already oozed.

Jasper crawled around Vin and moved from the sparse cover of a water butt, with not much water, to the cover that the younger brother had been using and did not need any more.

This was an abandoned haycart, leaning on two wheels, one of these smashed beyond repair. Vin had been crouched behind this and must have been facing front. But he had got hit from the side. Jasper wriggled around, trying to look in three directions at once.

There was nothing to see now. There was nothing to shoot at. There was, in fact, no more shooting. Not right now. No more hoofbeats. Just the soughing of the breeze.

From the centre of the settlement somebody shouted what sounded like a question. Nobody answered it.

Jasper could see Ginger, who seemed to be motionless.

The red-headed brother was behind what looked like a broken-down horse trough, but which could have been a doorless privy toppled by the wind at some earlier time and had been chewed since then incessantly by the elements.

Jasper could only see Ginger's lean butt and part of his shoulder and his arm. He was relieved when the man showed more of himself, looked at him.

120

'Vin?' It was a plaintive question.

'He's dead, Ginger. Stopped one in the head. Could hardly have known what hit him.'

'Hell,' said Ginger softly.

The horses started up again so suddenly that both men were taken by surprise, staring at each other with wide eyes, their mouths half-open. The hoofbeats came from behind them now, the sound rising to a crescendo. And then they were literally pinned down by a hail of lead.

Jasper heard Ginger scream something. He lost sight of the man, was rolling, slugs kicking the dust up around him.

Coming momentarily the right way round he fired at gun-flashes in the darkness. He felt something pluck at his arm, then he was rolling some more, not able to use his gun. He reached the shelter of a small feed-barn and, scrabbling up to his knees released the pin that held the door shut. He crawled through and pulled the door to behind him.

Outside the shooting had stopped as suddenly as it had begun and there was not even the sound of horses. But Jasper's head sang.

He wondered whether he was hit anywhere. He did not think so. He knew that, in the heat of battle even a serious wound might go unnoticed for a moment of time.

There had been no impact, no great kick or blow; and now no pain came.

He began to crawl again.

He was stiff and bruised, but he had no wounds, and his gun was still gripped in his hand.

He found Hack; for this was where Vin had dragged him after they had tied him up and gagged him.

Jasper peered at Hack and held his finger to his lips in a gesture of silence. Hack nodded his head to show that he understood.

Jasper removed his old cell-mate's gag and, producing his knife cut the bonds too. He handed Hack his gun, which he—Jasper—had insisted he had from Vin, who had wanted to see Hack dead anyway.

Jasper hissed, 'It went haywire, pard. We weren't such curly wolves as we'd figured. Vin's dead. I think they might have got Ginger as well. They're hunting us now, Hack, you an' me. Are you with me?'

'I'm with you now, Jasper.'

Gun in hand, Jasper began to move back towards the door. Hack scrabbled to his side, grabbed his arm.

'It's too damn' quiet out there. I figure that those skunks are out there just waiting and if you open that door you're gonna walk into a hail of lead. I think there's a way out at the back here. . . .'

'There ain't any door or window.'

'No, but there are gaps. You can see 'em. While the shooting was going on I saw the gun-flashes. Come on.'

Jasper turned about.

CHAPTER SEVENTEEN

Pete Ricken found himself in the vicinity of the other side's cover and gun in hand he crawled forward.

He almost ran into one of the two brothers, who had been shot in the side of the head.

Then he heard noises and he swivelled, stiffening, expecting lead to be thrown in his direction.

Somebody moaned.

It was a hatless ginger-headed man, the other brother.

He had a bullet in his chest. He was dying.

There was nothing Pete could do for him. But the elderly troubleshooter had to get away from the noises the man was making, which might draw shots in that direction.

Pete crawled some more. There were two other men and they could be in hiding. Jasper and his friend! There were plenty of places around here where they could be crouching.

Fugitive sounds escaped from the middle of the settlement, but there was nothing else.

Pete's spine began to prickle; the hairs at the nape of his neck stood on end.

Where was Toledo?

Pete became concerned for his partner. He began to crawl back the way he had come. I'll wear my knees to the bone, he thought. But he didn't feel like laughing; not even crying. Death seemed to be all around him. He felt soured and old.

A man was propped motionless against a hitching post.

Pete Ricken lay flat on his belly and became motionless too.

The other man did not move.

Pete began to wriggle forward on his belly. Hell's bells, he thought, I'm goin' to *scuff* myself to death.

He knew that form! It was Toledo. He looked like a sleeping Indian. But he wasn't just asleep!

Pete got onto his knees again and finished the rest of his abortive journey in double-quick time.

Toledo was still breathing, but with difficulty it seemed. He had been hit high up in the side. When Pete hissed his name, he made no move, no sign.

Desperately, Pete looked about him. He saw nothing. Then he heard the sound of hooves. Two horses, he thought. Was that those other two owlhooters getting away? He discovered he didn't really care one way or the other.

Now people began to move slowly into the street. Pete took a chance. 'Give me a hand over here,' he called.

Three men helped him to get Toledo into the saloon.

The half-breed began to moan with returning consciousness.

The old horse-doctor was half-inebriated as usual, but he was better than nothing.

Later, the old man told Pete that the elder brother Latch, on hearing the shooting had got up to try and help his two younger brothers. He had fallen down the stairs. He was unconscious. The old doctor did not think that Latch would ever regain consciousness; soon perhaps he would join his brothers in the morgue.

Ginger, the second brother to be shot, had died before he could be given any help. That bunch had not reckoned with the reckless bravery of the two men they had opposed. With extra fire-power they had thought they had the edge.

But their deaths didn't help Toledo none . . . .

The old sawbones said that if the bullet was not taken out of Toledo he would surely die.

But it was an operation that the old man himself could not possibly attempt.

Toledo was conscious, but he was not talking much.

Pete Ricken made his decision. He said:

'Hell, I'm not a lawman anymore. I don't carry a badge. I'm just a hired hand, a paid troubleshooter, a gunslinger. I don't have to get those men for the law. To hell with them! They didn't kill anybody when they pulled that job. Killers they might be, but what they did before is outside my jurisdiction—I'm no marshal, my badge-toting days are over and it's time my gun-toting ones were too. I'm taking you home, oldtimer, I'm getting you doctored properly.'

It was doubtful whether Toledo heard this speech at all. He certainly could not argue with it.

The settlement was all help now. The three killers that had held it in thrall were finished... A buckboard was produced, blankets, ropes.

Well-blanketed, Toledo was lashed securely into the buckboard. Everything was done to ensure that, on rough parts of the trail the discomfort he might suffer was cut to the minimum.

His horse and Pete's horse were tethered to the back of the buckboard so that they could trot behind. Pete got up on the seat, shook the reins. He said *Adios* and pulled away.

A hostler had told Pete that the two men who had fled had taken the same direction he had taken. That was a bit worrying. He did not want to be bushwhacked on the trail....

He needn't have worried.

To have heard a short conversation which took place between the two owlhooters as they left the settlement would have put Pete's mind at rest.

Jasper said: 'We'll make a detour and come around the other side. I figure that quick-shooting old bastard and his Injun friend 'ull think we've gone right on, that being the direction we were going in the first place. I figure we can fool 'em good if we double-back and return to Mainsville, or go back that way sort of.'

'All right,' said Hack.

'You'd want to go back to Mainsville I know,' said Jasper.

'Maybe. But how about that marshal? You figured he might get your stripe.'

'That's a chance we'd have to take, I'd have to take. If we actually go into Mainsville.'

'I'm beginning to feel like a goddam shuttlecock,' said Hack with an unusual show of petulance. 'I wisht you'd make your goddam mind up.'

He doesn't want to seem to be eager, thought Jasper, grinning to himself in the darkness . . . .

Maybe he, Jasper, could wait outside town while Hack went in and picked up that red-headed filly they called Missy. Would she go away with Hack? Well, you never could tell with women!

'Lead the way,' said Hack. 'But let's keep away from the trail we used before.'

'Sure, old hoss.'

127

I guess he's thinking of my neck too, thought Jasper.

Like ships that pass in the night without sight or signal Marshal Jack Muldoon and Jasper and Hack passed each other.

They did not see each other. They did not hear each other. The hard-bitten elderly lawman. And the pair. The pair of owlhooters, one of whom had a price on his head.

It was not an unusual thing in this wild, wide, far-stretching land; the passing, the *missing*. Brother missed brother. Cousin missed cousin. The pursued evaded the pursuer by a wind's breath. Trails were higgledy-piggledy and indistinct and settlements in some parts were very few and far between.

A man could spend years looking for a place or a person or both. Settlements rose quickly and disappeared almost as quickly. Even if their buildings had been fairly substantial, what had once been a thriving settlement could quickly become a 'ghost town', a cluster of wood and clapboard and wattle and logs and tin shelters battered by the weather and ravaged by predators.

There were towns that prospered and flourished and where, ultimately, folks lived in peace for most of their lives. There were towns

128

that became cities.

There were places that became famous and there were places that became notorious. And over them wandered a shifting population, for the West was the land of the wanderer, of hunters and hunted, of predator and prey, of the hard-working and the shiftless, the simple and the crooked.

There were so many degrees of people and things—and sometimes, as was the case with 'straight' oldsters like Pete Ricken and Marshal Muldoon, a man just did what he felt he had to do. It was the simplest way, if not always the easiest. . . .

And people passed in the night like vessels forever seeking an ideal port and never quite finding it and moving on, moving on . . . .

★   ★   ★

The fever came upon Jasper very suddenly and more fiercely than he had experienced anything before.

He doubled in the saddle, his breath leaving him in a great hiss of pain as something like red-hot talons tore at his belly.

In the darkness, Hack did not at first see his friend's discomfort. Then Jasper's head began to swim and he swayed in the saddle, only just saving himself from pitching out of it.

Then Hack turned his head. 'What's the

129

matter with you. You weren't hit were you?'

'No.' Jasper's words came out in a strangled form. 'It's that old sickness I guess. Like when you found me that night. The bug must still be in my system.'

'We'll light down,' said Hack. 'I'll brew some coffee. We'll have a smoke.'

'Yeh, mebbe if I can get outta this saddle for a bit . . . .'

'That looks like some trees up ahead. Can you make it?'

'I can make it.'

A little later, in the trees Hack had a small fire burning. Jasper lay in his poncho. He was trying to smoke but had twice dropped his cigarette. He was beginning to shake.

Hack took him a cup of coffee. He could not hold the cup steady himself. Hack held it for him while he cursed weakly, apologizing, and some of the liquid ran down his chin.

'Try an' get some shut-eye,' Hack said and turned back to the fire.

He hunkered down by the small flames. The night was still. There had been no signs of pursuit and he did not think there had been any. But there could be a search.

Jasper and he were pretty exposed out here; and Jasper would be about as much help as a fart to fight a thunderstorm.

He could see Jasper shaking now, the tremors becoming more violent all the time, so that he almost seemed to be throwing himself about where he lay. He mumbled curses.

Then, quite suddenly he began to shout.

The unintelligible noises awakened echoes in the night. And Hack knew how sounds carried on the breeze in the wild wideness of the prairies!

Hack rose and stamped out the fire. He went over to Jasper again. 'I'll have to get you to Mainsville, get you some medical attention. I'm gonna tie you to your saddle.'

Jasper did not seem to hear him.

Hack almost had to drag him.

CHAPTER EIGHTEEN

A middle-aged night clerk whom Hack had not seen before was on duty in the hotel-lobby. He was sleepy and not over-helpful. But when Hack stroked his palm with some long green he was more amenable, even when ordered to do so helping Hack to carry Jasper upstairs. They were able to have the big room they had shared the last time they stayed in the Mainsville Hotel.

The clerk directed Hack to the nearest doctor. Hack said there was no need to worry anybody else at this time of night—early morning actually—but a doctor he must have, for Jasper was in a sort of a coma now.

131

The clerk said he was glad the man wasn't shot: Missy would not like him letting a shot man in here, not without telling her first anyway. Hack told the man that Missy was a friend of his and, *whatever*, he would fix it with her.

Privately, he hoped he could call the beautiful red-headed hotel-keeper a friend; maybe more ere long.

The clerk said he hoped that what Hack's friend had wrong with him was not catching. Hack said that Jasper had had this sort of thing before while he, Hack, had ridden along with him. And Hack hadn't caught anything, felt as fit as a skunk.

He went down the street and rousted out the doctor, a tall grey-faced man, who suffered from insomnia anyway and was sitting browsing through Eastern medical magazines and drinking bourbon and water when Hack disturbed him.

He was mellow but not drunk. Getting his black bag, he said he'd be glad to see a case of honest-to-goodness sickness: he had seen too many brawling scars and knife and gunshot wounds lately. This town seemed to be getting kind of wild all of a sudden. He gave Hack sidelong glances as if he thought the lean young man might have had something to do with this new state of affairs—and he could have been right at that.

132

Was the owlhoot brand growing, Hack wondered, the brand that he could not see, but other folk seemed to spot on him?

He didn't remember the doctor. But maybe the doctor remembered him, or had heard of him and his companion.

Reaching the room where Jasper lay, the medico was, however, all efficiency, and Hack knew his pard was in good hands. The doc gave Jasper a draught of something and the shaking man was soon still, and then he slept.

The doctor gave Hack a bottle of brown evil-smelling stuff and said:

'I'll be back to see him at about eleven a.m. but if he awakes before that give him two big spoonfuls of this.'

'Sure, Doc.'

The stooping grey-faced man took his leave.

Hack undressed and got into the other bed. He knew that the built-in clock he carried in his head would awaken him before eleven, even if he was tired enough to sleep that long. He was soon away, breathing deeply and evenly, and Jasper making no ugly sounds now to disturb him.

★   ★   ★

The day-clerk who turned up that morning was the one who had signed-in Jasper and Hack at the hotel on their first visit to Mainsville. From his night-colleague's description of the two men he was able to identify them and he told the older man about them.

The night-man said: 'Yeh, I heard about them, about that shindig. I was away at my sister's at the time, you may remember, Jimmy.'

'Yes, I remember,' said Jimmy.

'I had an idea those two were gunslingers. Do you think the sick one might be wounded someplace after all?'

'Could be,' said Jimmy. 'Those two certainly are a couple of shooting fools. I know them!'

'Watch the desk, Hank,' he added importantly. 'I'll go report to Missy.'

'Don't be long,' said the disgruntled older man. 'I want my breakfast.'

Missy was in the kitchen and she received Jimmy's report with interest. But she finally said, 'Let them sleep.'

Jimmy returned to Hank. 'Missy says to let 'em be.'

'I'm off to my breakfast,' said Hank.

That young jasper is getting too big for his boots, he thought. And, after breakfast he took himself a pasear down to the marshal's office.

He was surprised to learn that Marshal Jack Muldoon was not there. But he was also surprised at peg-legged Deputy Jeremiah's reaction to the news he had brought.

Hank was curious. But the oldster, Jeremiah, did not satisfy Hank's curiosity. Hank went home to bed. Jeremiah sat in the swivel chair behind the law-office desk and did some cogitating.

Jack had gone out after those two. He must have missed them somehow. Unless they had drygulched him, left him out on the plain. But would they have dared to come to Mainsville afterwards, a place where questions were bound to be asked?

One of them was sick anyway: did that have something to do with it? It must have, Jeremiah thought . . . .

He was acting-lawman here now. He knew what he had to do.

★   ★   ★

When Hack awoke and sat up in his bed there was an apparition sitting at the other end of it, on a chair pulled up to the bottom of the bed.

Hack was not sure at first of the nature of the apparition. But nearer to him than the apparition itself and held by said apparition was something the nature of which Hack had no difficulty at all in identifying. The twin barrels of the sawn-off shotgun looked like black, wicked eyes and they were staring right at him.

'I've got your gun-rig, bucko,' the apparition said. 'Don't make any quick moves or I'm liable to blow your head off.'

And at that distance he wasn't bragging.

'Hallo, Jeremiah,' said Hack weakly, recognizing his visitor at last. During Hack's fairly recent sojourn in the Mainsville jail he and Jeremiah had had a few chinwags together.

He had liked the old goat, had thought him harmless, had never expected to see him in such a warlike pose—particularly with himself, Hack, taking the tacky end of the stick.

But nobody pointed a loaded shotgun at a friend!

And where was Marshal Muldoon?

He asked where Marshal Muldoon was, and Jeremiah explained about this; and the reason for the old deputy's warlike pose became clearer to Hack, though none the less fraught.

In the other bed, Jasper began to stir and mutter.

'I'd better go look at him,' Hack said.

'All right then . . . But easy now.'

The eyes of the shotgun followed Hack's progress closely, never deviating by a fraction.

Jasper looked a lot better. His brow was not sweat-bedewed; his face was smooth.

As the doctor had said—and Hack knew this from his own experience with Jasper—the fever could flare up violently at any time but could just as easily abate.

But old Jeremiah would not know this!

Somebody rapped on the door.

Jeremiah rose and moved away from the bed so that Hack could get past him, so that there

136

was a clear gap between both of them and the door.

Jeremiah jerked the muzzle of the shotgun slightly. 'See who it is. Go very very easy.'

Bare-footed and in his long johns, Hack padded over to the door and opened it.

'Oh, hallo, Doc!'

The doctor said: 'I'm earlier than I planned. But I had a sudden call to the hotel, a fat drummer with stomach trouble. He had just eaten too much supper I think, including something that disagreed with him. I thought I would take the opportunity to call on my other patient while I was here.'

★   ★   ★

In some parts of the West there were as many doctors as there were lawmen, though probably not so many of them as there was of the lawless breed.

But because of the lawless breed and their depredations—as well as genuine accidents that happened to hard-working folk who worked with tools and with animals—doctors always had some kind of work. And, as there were all kinds of laymen and their wives and daughters, so there were literally all kinds of doctors.

Some very good medical men who had had first-class training abroad or back East and were sick of administering pretty-coloured draughts to fretful businessmen and their bored wives and daughters and travelled to answer the challenge of the wild places of the new land, the far West. Some of them prospered; some of them, after a time of tribulations, were glad to return from whence they came.

And there were of course the *other kind*. Doctors, yes; but bad doctors, or doctors that had been found guilty of criminal practices or misconduct. Some of them had been 'struck off'. But it was easy for them to hang their shingle in some godforsaken cowtown or mining camp.

Some of them redeemed themselves and became respected members of the community, albeit under an assumed name. Others never changed. They treated illicit gunshot wounds and manglings caused by dangerous weapons or boots or human teeth. They sold illicit drugs to whores and psychopaths. They were called out to succour Wanted men in outlaw hide-outs. They feathered their mucky nests in any way they could.

Some of them were not even doctors. They were vets and apothecaries and ex-drug-store assistants and chemists and confidence men and charlatans who sold coloured water in gaudily-labelled bottles. Some of them, like the notorious 'Doc' Holliday of Tombstone, were merely dentists . . . .

But Jasper, abed in the Mainsville Hotel, had

a good doctor.

And when, with his friend troubleshooter Pete Ricken, the half-Indian Toledo got back to base, he had a good doctor too.

The rich mine-owners could afford to hire a good man to look after their workers and the staff. If a man was sick he could not work—and to these people work and profit was of the essence of life.

'He's going to be all right, Pete,' said the little fat man in a white coat as he dropped a battered bullet with a 'clank' into a tin pan at Toledo's bedside.

'That slug didn't touch anything vital. He has no fever—but he has got the constitution of a pack mule. It's a good thing you brought him home right away though.'

'Couldn't do anything else,' grumbled the walrus-moustached troubleshooter, always made uncomfortable by anything resembling praise.

In the bed, half-awake, Toledo was cursing cheerfully to himself in perfect English.

CHAPTER NINETEEN

In the room in the hotel in Mainsville, the tall grey-faced man who tended the sick in that salubrious township was gazing about him with astonishment.

'These ginks are under arrest, Doc,' said Deputy Jeremiah, his shotgun pointed at Hack's belly. 'Howmsoever, I reckon you ought to be able to take a look at the sick one.'

'A sick man is a sick man,' said the doctor severely. 'Under arrest or not.'

'I reckon,' said Jeremiah laconically. 'But just stay right where you are for a mite longer, will yuh, Doc?' The peglegged oldster levelled his wicked-looking gun at Hack.

'You take the two gun-rigs and place 'em over there by the window.' He jerked his head. But the shotgun-muzzle did not waver.

Hack took all the armaments belonging to Jasper and himself and put them where Jeremiah had said and then, in that large room, they were all separated from everybody present.

'All right, Doc,' said Jeremiah. 'Tend to your patient.'

What none of them knew was that the patient, in the nature of his illness, was far better than was expected and knew everything that was going on around him.

Jeremiah and the good doctor did not know that Jasper was in the habit of keeping his knife by him at all times, particularly when he slept. And Hack had forgotten this also. Things were happening too fast!

Right now Jasper had the knife under his pillow.

And things were about to happen even faster.

The doctor bent over his patient and then turned away to open his little black bag and delve into it as it lay where he had put it on the wooden chair beside the bed.

The man in the bed rose swiftly, his knife in his left hand; with his right he grabbed the doctor across the chest from behind and pulled him backwards.

Then the blade of the knife was pressed to the doctor's throat.

'Keep still,' Jasper said, 'or you're a dead man.'

His empty hands raised from the bag, the doctor froze.

The other two men were still also, their eyes mirroring shocked surprise. Even Jasper's friend, Hack looked as if he were being suddenly menaced too.

And Jeremiah, half-crouching, held his shotgun forward but did nothing. He did not want to blow his friend the doctor to Kingdom Come. Agonies of indecision were mirrored on the old lawman's wizened face as he faced the outlaw and his human shield.

'Put the shotgun on the floor, old man,' said Jasper. 'Or, I promise you, your favourite sawbones will be as dead as dead meat can be.'

Slowly, carefully, and with the cautious stiffness of age, Jeremiah bent and put the shotgun on the floor at his feet.

'Now step away from it!'

Jeremiah stepped back.

'Pick it up, Hack, and prop it against the wall by the door.'

'If you say so, Jasper.' Keeping well out of the way of the choleric old deputy who looked as if he were about to explode, Hack carried out Jasper's order.

'Now collect the gun-rigs so that you'll have plenty o' fire-power.'

Hack did this too, draping the cartridge-belts over his shoulder, keeping one gun in his hand to dissuade Jeremiah from any foolish move.

But the oldster seemed now to have resigned himself. His wrinkled face was set, impassive.

Jasper let the doctor go, pushed him to one side.

'You're fools,' the tall man said. 'Both of you.'

'Just stay still, Doc,' Jasper said. 'Keep 'em covered, Hack.'

'I'm doing that, ain't I?' said Hack irritably.

Jasper climbed into his clothes.

Hack said: 'Ain't it about time I got dressed too?'

'Oh, sure.'

Fully dressed, Jasper took his gunbelt from Hack and strapped it on. Then, gun in hand and the other belt draped over his shoulder he covered the deputy and the doctor while Hack took his turn in getting ready.

142

Soon they were ready; both with a gun in his hand. But, at the door Jasper holstered his Colt and picked up the shotgun. Half-crouching, he pointed this at Jeremiah. His lips drew back slowly from his teeth.

'I'm gonna blow your belly out, ol' man,' he said.

And, in that shocked moment, the other men there knew that Jasper meant exactly what he said.

With his free hand, Hack caught hold of the barrel of the long gun and forced it upwards. Momentarily, Jasper resisted the pressure and there was a danger that he might, even involuntarily, squeeze the trigger.

Jeremiah and the doctor were tense, their eyes wide. And Jeremiah, looking death in the face, had completely lost his impassivity. He looked as if he was about to shout something. But he did not. He could not risk a move, a spring, for even while grasping the shotgun Hack still had his Colt pointed at the two men.

And the yawning muzzles of the shotgun were only slowly rising, going out of line.

But Hack was stronger than Jasper.

And suddenly Jasper's bones and sinews seemed to go fluid and Hack took the long gun from him and balanced it in his one hand, his six-gun in the other. And like a man in a dream Jasper took out his own belt-gun and pointed it in the same direction as Hack was doing. Was he going to fire this? But then Hack glanced quickly at his partner and said in a soft, thick voice, 'What's the matter with you—have you gone kill-crazy or somep'n?'

Jasper did not reply. His eyes were yellow and had a lost look about them; they were red-rimmed. Jasper was not so well again as he had thought he was.

'Move,' said Hack, and Jasper moved.

He opened the door and passed through it.

Following him, Hack propped the shotgun against the hall wall as he changed the doorkey from one side of the door to the other. He said:

'I shouldn't do anything hasty if I were you, gents. I can't guarantee anything—and I don't think any of us want shooting that might endanger innocent people, do we?'

Neither of the two men in the room answered him. They just stared at him.

He closed the door and locked it on the outside. He threw the key through the open window at the end of the hall and then he followed Jasper down the stairs.

Hack pouched his hand-gun, but he kept the shotgun at ready.

Jasper held his Colt in front of him as he led the way down the stairs.

The day-clerk, young Jimmy, was behind the desk in the lobby. His eyes bugged when he saw the two armed men coming down the stairs and he recognized them. A lot was going on that he did not understand and he was getting scared.

'You got a gun under there, son?' said Hack.

Jimmy shook his head furiously from side to side, no sounds coming from his open lips.

'Move out!'

Jimmy moved out from behind the desk and Hack had a quick look-see. The boy seemed to be telling the truth.

'Stay quiet like a mouse,' Hack said and this time Jimmy nodded his head like a puppet instead of shaking it.

Jasper was already on his way through the swing doors into the street.

Trepidation started to tug at Hack's nerve-ends.

He followed Jasper quickly.

There was something wild about Jasper now. As if his sickness had addled his brain. But maybe he had always been like that inside: a wild man while the chips were down.

The chips were not exactly *down* now.

But they still had to get out of this town with whole skins.

And Hack couldn't help hoping that nobody else got hurt while they were on their way out.

And then maybe Jasper would be better. . . .

CHAPTER TWENTY

Trails were crossed and re-crossed. Trails were obliterated by weather and others were made in their places, but there were always deviations. The earth changed and the people changed with it. Trails criss-crossed. People passed; went; sometimes they returned. Or a man could live in the same territory for all of his life and still get temporarily lost from time to time. He could even perish because, pulled into a false sense of security by the very familiarity of his wild surroundings, he did not allow for erratic conditions that could so quickly develop.

The area that a riding man called his 'territory' could, in fact, be enormously wide and be spreading all the time. Or, with encroaching civilization it could be shrinking; and not all hazards were elemental ones.

So all Western men became, in a sense, trackers. They used trails that an Easterner would not even be able to see; they scanned distances and found landmarks; they 'read sign'.

A working cowboy's ridings were limited to the area of his ranching activities. But, most cowboys, unless they landed themselves a peach of a job, were wont to 'fiddlefoot'. They knew the trails. Even the drummers who travelled the West selling all kinds of commodities strange or mundane knew the trails which gave less worry and wear to a four-footed beast; and some of these people had small carriages too. And there were the stage coaches and the prairie schooners and the chuck-wagons and the cathouse and circus wagons and the armoured prison equipages. But the lawmen ranged the widest, and the confidence men, and the outlaws and gamblers and professional gunfighters; sometimes a bit of each of these embodied in one man and making him a formidable mixture.

And of such a mixture was Marshal Jack Muldoon, now of Mainsville.

And Jack was a mighty fine tracker too.

The two boys who called themselves Jasper and Hack had been mighty clever. One of them at least was cunningly adept at covering tracks. That'd be Jasper, thought Muldoon.

But Jack himself had been back and forth between Mainsville and the sinkhole settlement run by bald-headed Latch and his two brothers many times and he knew every lump and pothole and stunted tree for miles around.

Hell had been raised in the settlement and men had been killed for whom no folk would mourn, least of all Marshal Muldoon. And Muldoon's quarry had gone out the other side.

But Muldoon had over the years schooled himself to think the way people of Jasper's stripe thought; his mind was as devious as Jasper's and he had an edge in age and

147

experience.

He had discovered that the two had doubled back.

He figured that they might be making for Mainsville.

He turned; and he picked up their trail again; and it was light and the morning went on.

★   ★   ★

Jimmy hammered on Missy's door and confronted her with the dire story.

She got her bunch of pass-keys and went along the hall and set Jeremiah and the doctor free from the locked room.

As they all trooped past the room occupied by fat, helpless Jacob Sanlee, he called out to know what was happening.

'Doc; Missy,' old Jeremiah said authoritatively. 'You go in there and stay with Jacob. Jimmy, you go back to your post at the desk. I have to go out there.'

'Jeremiah, you have no weapon,' the doctor said.

'Ask Jacob if I can borrow his rifle. Then do as I say. There's no time to waste.'

'All right, Jeremiah.'

Jimmy went downstairs. The doctor brought the rifle out to the old deputy. Missy was already telling her 'Uncle Jacob' what was going on. The doctor rejoined them. Missy seemed to be on the point of tears.

'Get over to the window, Doc,' said Jacob. 'Tell me what's happening now. It's mighty quiet out there.'

The tall stooped man went over to the window and peered around the curtains.

He said: 'They're just walking down the middle of the street. The older one's still got the shotgun, and the other's got a hand-gun. They're spaced out and looking about them. Nobody else is in sight. Everybody's taken cover I guess. I can't see Jeremiah yet.'

From his throne on the bed Jacob said: 'That old lawman's got more guts than a momma bobcat, but he isn't the sort to take fool chances. He could pick 'em off from the hotel. Come to think of it, he might have been able to pick 'em off from up here with that rifle of mine.'

The doctor said: 'I don't guess Jeremiah is the sort to do that.'

'No, I guess not.'

The doctor started to talk again, his voice rising excitedly.

'There's somebody else coming down the street, from the opposite direction... By all that's holy, it's the marshal! It's Jack Muldoon! He's back!'

★   ★   ★

The marshal had a gun in each hand and his

arms were extended almost at full length; but the heavy guns were straight and unwavering, one for each man as Muldoon strode slowly forward, an erect figure with hat pushed back from broad forehead, revealing a thick wing of iron-grey hair.

He had taken the two men completely by surprise. They had thought he was long gone. And now he was in good shooting distance.

He said clearly, 'That's far enough, boys. Drop your guns.'

But Jasper raised the shotgun.

Muldoon fired with both his guns, the reports sounding like the roll of small cannons.

Both bullets hit Jasper in the chest. The shotgun fell from his hands and clattered as it hit the hard surface of the street, raising little puffs of dust.

Jasper seemed to be trying to run backwards. But then his feet shot from under him and he fell flat on his back and the dust was thicker now.

Muldoon was down on one knee, the two guns still levelled.

'Don't make me kill you as well, boy,' he said.

Hack's gun was only half-raised. He glanced back at Jasper, lying flat in the dust, the blood already seeping from beneath his body where the heavy slugs had smashed through.

He looked back at the marshal and the

150

steadily levelled guns. He had seen some quick-draw artistes. But accurate shooting of that calibre was something else!

Then a voice behind him called, 'Better give up, Hackwood, I've got a rifle trained on your spine.'

That was old Jeremiah!

Hackwood let his gun slip from his hand. It hit the ground with a dull thud.

'I've got no quarrel with you, Marshal,' Hackwood said.

There was another voice calling then. But this time it was a female one.

'*Hack!*'

He turned slowly.

'I'm all right, Missy,' he said.

★ ★ ★

The prison wagon was a fair while coming in that it had to do a round trip and pick up other miscreants and Mainsville was one of its last ports of call.

In the meantime Jasper had been buried and his friend, Hack, under armed guard was allowed to attend the funeral; together with the marshal and his deputy, the doctor, Missy, and other assorted citizens and hangers-on. The service was, understandably, quite brief.

But eventually the prison equipage arrived and Hack was incarcerated with the others and

151

the long armour-plated barred-windowed vehicle rumbled away with its four horses. And Marshall Muldoon and his young, auburn-haired friend Missy stood in the trail looking after it.

The girl's beautiful face was tear-stained.

'It may not be as bad as you think, honey,' said Muldoon. 'In fact, I don't opine that it *will* be as bad as you think. So be optimistic.'

'I usually am,' the girl said, but her eyes were shadowed.

The elderly lawman looked at her and said: 'He's alive and he's healthy. I'm going to do my best for him at the trial, and there are some pretty helpful circumstances. He virtually saved Jeremiah's life, remember? Jeremiah will testify to that and so will the doctor, who said Jasper would surely have burned Jeremiah down with his own shotgun if Hack hadn't stopped him. . . .'

'I guess the man was sick in the head as well as in the body,' said Missy, softly.

'I guess that's the charitable way to look at it, and maybe you're right, honey. . . Anyway, we've got all the money back and I've been in touch by telegraph with the mine-owners whose payroll it was.' Muldoon's face split into a grin and the girl's face brightened at the look of it. And the marshal went on:

'They're sending a man to pick up the *dinero*. Turns out he's an old saddle pard o' mine. An ex-lawman. Name's Pete Ricken. Ain't seen him in a coon's age. He used to have the handsomest walrus moustache I've ever seen. Hope he's still got it. . . .

'Strangely enough, Pete was on the trail of Jasper and Hack to try and get the money back. Then Pete's pardner, a half-breed called Toledo, got himself shot-up and they had to turn back. I had all this in a letter from Pete only yesterday, way after I'd telegraphed. He'll be here himself in a few days. . . .'

'Your friend's friend, the half-breed called Toledo, is he all right?'

'He's fine. Seems he's part-Dutch. Ol' Pete sure writes a nice story-book-type letter. An' here's me allus thought he was illiterate.' Grinning some more, Muldoon nudged the girl's arm. 'Be patient, honey. Things are gonna be all right in the end, take that from your Uncle Jack. C'mon, let's get some coffee.'

They turned around and she took his hand the way she used to when she was a little sprig. Her steps became springier as they walked back to the hotel.

Photoset, printed and bound in Great Britain by REDWOOD BURN LIMITED, Trowbridge, Wiltshire